THE TURNING WHEEL

THE TURNING WHEEL

Christina Green

Chivers Press • G.K. Hall & Co.
Bath, England   Thorndike, Maine USA

This Large Print edition is published by Chivers Press, England, and by G.K. Hall & Co., USA.

Published in 2000 in the U.K. by arrangement with the author, care of Dorian Literary Agency.

Published in 2000 in the U.S. by arrangement with Dorian Literary Agency.

U.K. Hardcover ISBN 0-7540-4109-3 (Chivers Large Print)
U.K. Softcover   ISBN 0-7540-4110-7 (Camden Large Print)
U.S. Softcover   ISBN 0-7838-9000-1 (Nightingale Series Edition)

The text of this Large Print edition is unabridged.
Other aspects of the book may vary from the original edition.

Set in 16 pt. New Times Roman.

Printed in Great Britain on acid-free paper.

British Library Cataloguing in Publication Data available

Library of Congress Cataloging-in-Publication Data

Green, Christina.
  The turning wheel / by Christina Green.
      p.   cm.
  ISBN 0-7838-9000-1 (lg. print : sc : alk. paper)
  1. Family reunions—Fiction. 2. Devon (England)—Fiction.
  3. Water mills—Fiction. 4. Large type books. I. Title.
PR6057.R3378 T8   2000
823'.914—dc21   00–021443

CHAPTER ONE

Nicola Bennett swung the snarling little MG around in the last bend and then parked outside Aunt Rachel's holiday home, wondering what on earth she was doing here in Devon when by rights she should be working hard in London.

True, Devon was glorious on this early April morning, pale primroses dotting the narrow, twisting lanes that headed into the countryside beyond Exeter. The blue sky was a tonic after the last week of heavy showers which had dampened her spirits. Now she felt uplifted, even though deep inside her a querulous voice demanded, 'What about your job? Your home? You know you shouldn't be here.'

'Shut up,' she told it firmly, and then grinned as excitement surfaced once more, despite her reluctant agreement with that reprimanding whisper.

She was only here for a weekend, after all, a family reunion, hoped-for reconciliations and fresh relationships. What could be wrong with that?

London was a very long way away; so was her word processor, and the proofs of next year's Holiday Cottages Accommodation brochure waiting to be corrected.

For a second, gathering her mobile phone

and her canvas bag from the back of the car, Nicki paused. She grinned, tightening her grip around her mobile phone and quickly switched it off. No chance of anyone ringing, with an urgent job down here in the southwest, thank you very much! Her smile faded as a fleeting wish that someone cared enough to ring her stabbed through her mind. Since the last failed relationship a sense of loneliness had made itself felt.

Then suddenly a well-loved voice bit into her thoughts, and the regret faded.

'Nicki! My dearest girl!'

She turned, ran up the path, dropped her bag, and hugged Harry Bennett with an almost panic-stricken warmth, in case his presence was just another dream.

'Dad, it's so wonderful to see you. How are you?'

She stepped back, anxiously recalling how Geraldine had written from Canada about his angina, that he was frail and despondent and that he wanted only to come home, to England, to Devon.

'All the better for seeing you, my darling. I've forgotten all the bad times now.'

His bright hazel eyes were smiling, a little moist, she saw, with a pricking behind her own eyelids.

'It's been a very long time, Nicki.'

She linked her arm with his, feeling with an unsteady surge of emotion the weakness of his

2

body. Dad had always been so strong, tall and well-built; her childhood hero, who had made it so hard for her to put another man in his place. Even now, aged twenty-seven, among numerous boyfriends, she had not yet found a replacement for him.

She smiled into his perceptive eyes, noted the circles of pouchy flesh beneath them, felt his feet stumbling slightly, as they walked towards the open door and said warmly, 'We'll make this a weekend to remember, Dad. No worries, nothing but just being together.'

His arm pressed into her side.

'All I want,' he said quietly, and she saw the old vigour momentarily return to his thin face.

Then her stepmother, Geraldine, was on the doorstep, her white hair an exuberant halo of curls, slim figure elegant and trendy, brilliant eyes assessing and weighing up as ever.

'Darling Nicki!'

The high, almost childlike voice with its slight transatlantic twang, hadn't changed over the years she and Dad had been away. Nicki smiled, but didn't waste energy on trying to reply. She knew that Gee, as she was best known, would carry on her usual monologue as long as she wished. Yet, despite her normal self-confidence, Nicki found she was thinking like a child again, wishing she'd dressed up for the occasion. Stone-coloured linen trousers and the old chunky sweater were hardly up to Gee's immaculate standard. But it didn't matter. Gee was in full flight again.

'Harry's been so impatient, waiting for this moment, that I've hardly been able to restrain him from jogging down to the crossroads to meet you! Come in, honey. Leave your bag, oh, and your phone. Of course we're all on mobiles now, aren't we? I'll go and put the kettle on. Only homespun technology here, I guess!'

They followed her hurrying figure along the passage and into the little conservatory that opened off the dining-room at the back of the cottage.

'Sit down! Harry can bring you up to date while I make coffee—a woman's role, you know, Nicki. He sits and chats while I do the chores. Nothing changes! Ah, well.'

Brief laughter pealed, and Harry gave Nicki a wry smile as she collapsed in the cane chair he held for her.

So nothing's altered, she reflected, and knew he shared the thought. But this weekend she wouldn't let Gee's subtle mischief upset her. This, as Dad had said, was to be a weekend to remember, a family weekend. And something else. Nicki's thoughts were busy. What had Gee's scribbled postscript said on that last letter?

'We've got a brilliant idea, a new project. Leo is involved, and so are you, my girl. Be prepared!'

Leo Forman, Gee's only son by her previous

marriage, arrived just as lunch was being served. Nicki, carrying a colourful salad dressed with marigolds and borage from Aunt Rachel's famous cottage garden, caught her breath as she heard his voice. It was light and easy, just as she remembered it, still infinitely attractive.

After he'd greeted his mother, he came into the conservatory, and Nicki gave him the careful smile she'd been preparing. Handsome as ever, in his careless way, dressed in chinos and a patterned shirt that shouted tasteful individuality. Yes, Leo Forman was just as she remembered him. How long ago had they parted? Too long for it to matter now.

But Nicki's thoughts instantly somersaulted into the past. She'd been a gauche seventeen-year-old school-leaver, and sophisticated Leo was already approaching twenty-one when she'd fallen for him. She recalled that early summer when the world had seemed full of surprises and happiness, those carefree days when she had truly thought Leo was the man for her, until he'd whisked off to the States to build a prize-winning office block and embarked on his secondary career of loving other women.

Now Nicki tightened her lips and met his gaze with resolute serenity. She might still feel a few flickerings of the old emotion she had taken for love, but she was older now—older, wiser, and with a built-in second skin that had made her a survivor where men were concerned.

'Here he is!'

Gee's tinkling laughter filled the small silence in which they stared at each other.

'Your old childhood sweetheart, home again. Great to have him back, isn't it?'

Nicki ignored the question in her stepmother's words and smiled coolly into Leo's amused eyes, assessing her so critically.

'How are you, Leo?'

She hoped the few, slightly formal words would set a new relationship between them. She had no wish to pick up old strings, despite Gee's obvious expectation.

He was at her side, smiling, nodding, the devastating twinkle very evident. He hadn't changed much. Well, she had. Nicki turned away and replaced the salad bowl on a different spot on the crowded table.

'I'm fine, just great.' He'd acquired a slight Canadian accent. 'And how about you, Nicko?'

The old name. She fidgeted, but he continued, not waiting for an answer.

'You know what? You've turned into a beauty. I guess the tomboy's gone? Sad, but, hey, I'm impressed.'

Gratefully, she responded to the well-remembered teasing mode.

'Rubbish. I've still got freckles and I bet I could still run you to a standstill.'

He laughed, moving towards Harry who sat

6

beside the open door, but still looking at her over his shoulder.

'Moody little scrap, weren't you? But I reckon you've grown up a bit now. Mother tells me you work for a national holiday company and dash around the country in that neat little motor outside. Boyfriends, galore, too, no doubt.'

And then, before she could come back with a smart comment on his own, extremely free-ranging life style, he was shaking Harry's hand.

'Hi there, Harry,' he said then listened intently to the answering tired voice, seemingly full of affectionate concern.

But Nicki, watching, remembered past scenes when she had learned that Leo's famous charm had masked a deeper, only half-concealed disregard of others' problems, and felt herself grow tense again.

She did so hope that this weekend visit wasn't heralding a repeat of past conflicts that she had believed long gone. Her mind darkened as momentarily she recalled that brief, wild involvement with Leo, and her longfelt distrust of his doting mother.

'Harry's taking a nap,' Gee said after lunch, returning to the conservatory where Nicki and Leo sat, drinking coffee and catching up on the recent past. 'All this excitement isn't good for him. He gets so worked up. He'll be fine again when he's rested.'

Her eyes gleamed with excitement, and

7

Nicki thought warily, here it is, the famous project she wrote to her about. But why does it have to be talked about now, when Dad's not here? Does that mean he doesn't approve? Perhaps he doesn't even know about it. Typical of Gee to be so secretive.

'Hurry up and finish your coffee, honey! We're off on a visit. It'll only take ten minutes there and ten minutes back, and Harry always sleeps for at least an hour. Come on, what's keeping you two?'

Gee was out of the conservatory, in the hall, flinging on an anorak and jingling her car keys before Nicki caught up with her.

'What are you talking about?' she demanded, feeling a stab of the old irritation.

Gee was always pushing people about.

'Where do we have to go, and why? And why when Dad's asleep?'

She heard the edge in her voice and regretted it. This wasn't the time to get on the wrong side of Gee but, just like her son, Gee hadn't changed. She was still intent on having her own way, of manipulating everyone. Yet her smile, as she looked over her shoulder, already halfway down the garden path, was blandly reassuring.

'It's OK, honey, I'm not doing a double-deal on your dad. He knows all about it, and we'll discuss everything when he's up again. Now, come on! We'll take the Land-Rover, room for us all. Leo, what are you waiting for?'

8

Gee's driving, Nicki thought grimly, jerking about in the vehicle as her stepmother careered down the lanes, hadn't improved over the years.

'Guess where we're off to?' Gee asked cheerfully, as a straight piece of road appeared. 'You know the place from 'way back. Didn't we have summer picnics there with Rachel when we were all on vacation together?'

Nicki's mind was abruptly full of remembered images. She recalled Aunt Rachel, sharing the cottage with them that summer, at least ten years ago. Nicki had been a defiant teenager, Leo at his most arrogantly charming, and Dad had been strong, healthy, full of fun. In her mind she heard his voice, as they looked around them, at the favourite picnic place.

'A wicked shame to let this old place fall down. Wouldn't I just love to have a hand in restoring it? What a challenge it would be.'

His eagerness had caught Nicki's attention, but now, Gee was slowing down, driving through a dilapidated gateway, parking the Land-Rover beneath a clump of old beech trees.

'This is it, remember, Nicki? You used to call it Bluebell Mill because of the flowers, and Rachel painted it. We all had terrific fun with barbecues, and fishing in the stream.'

'OK, Ma. We get the picture,' Leo replied,

his voice gentle but firm.

Glancing at him as she climbed out of the vehicle, Nicki was surprised at his expression as their eyes met. So he remembered, too. This had been the place of their first kiss, beneath the willow trees, lower down the stream. It had been a magical moment that she'd forgotten until now. Looking at him, she saw the intentness of his gaze and wondered at his thoughts.

Frowning, she walked quickly towards the millhouse. It was a near-derelict ruin, its weathered boards grey and lichen-covered, the tall broken chimney an ugly pile of shattered red bricks. She turned, going towards the side of the house where she knew the wheelpit used to be. Gee was saying something to Leo, just behind her, but she didn't listen. She must find out about the wheel. For some reason, it was vital to know if it was still there, if it still turned.

'Can I help you?'

The low, vibrant voice broke into her thoughts and she twisted around. A tall man stood at the doorway of the millhouse, staring at her. A dark stubble outlined his uncompromisingly strong chin, and his dark tousled hair needed cutting. He wore ancient jeans, and a black polo-necked sweater with snags up and down the baggy sleeves. In his left hand he carried some sort of tool.

But it was his eyes that caught her attention.

They were light blue, pale and unblinking, as if he could see right into her. Feeling uncharacteristically foolish, Nicki fumbled for words, but it was Gee who answered him as she approached.

'Hi, Mr Armstrong! I've brought my son to see the property.'

She held out her hand and smiled flirtatiously. Nicki, standing where she was, watched the little scene with unexpected trepidation. Gee was going to eat up this man, she knew it, and suddenly everything became clear. This was the project, something Dad had wanted years ago, and now Gee had decided to take it upon herself, including Leo, of course, to make the old mill into—what?

Nicki imagined a place where Gee could boastfully invite her friends for weekends. The wheel would turn again, but not for its original reason. She could almost hear Gee.

'Hey, just look at this old wheel! Isn't it the cutest thing you've ever seen? Hasn't Leo been absolutely brilliant, making it work again, giving the place that funny old look? My clever boy!'

Nicki felt an urgency grow inside her. She wouldn't let her devious stepmother get away with such desecration. Grealy Mill was centuries old, a wonderful relic of past days, past ways. Surely it deserved better than a stylish make-over such as she intuitively knew Gee was planning. She stepped forward, saw

11

the man called Armstrong slowly take Gee's hand, reluctantly, she thought, and then listen to what Gee was saying.

Unable to stop herself, Nicki interrupted Gee. 'The wheel,' she said rapidly, looking up at the man's strong face, and finding herself suddenly the target of those amazingly light eyes, 'is it still working? Can I go round and look? I hope you don't mind.'

She felt Gee and Leo staring at her, but she went on regardless.

'It's important,' she finished tersely.

'Of course I don't mind. The wheel's not turning, I'm afraid. There's not enough water to power it. But the pit's overgrown, and the edge is a bit shaky. Take care where you tread.'

He spoke with a pleasant baritone voice, gravelly, with a hint of a gentle Devon accent. Nicki nodded and turned away.

The wheelpit was as ruined as he had warned. She made her way through willow saplings, soggy carpets of beech leaves remaining from last winter, and a green tangle of newly emerging ferns, to stand at last beside the vast, motionless wheel. It resembled a decaying monument, she thought unhappily, its old vigour long dead. Now the mill stream had become a puddled trickle of stagnant water, its chuckling voice gone, along with its energy and driving power.

Nicki remembered, with stabbing clarity, the

12

noise that had always been part of the wheel and its constant drive. It used to creak as it turned, filling the whole building with its movement and accompanying humming song. And she recalled the splashing, as the buckets worked their way through the churning water, scooping up the energy, and then returning it into the stream, to rush away over the millrace, finally mingling once again with the nearby river.

She wasn't aware of how long she'd stood there, thinking back, thinking forward, wondering what all this was about, and aware that she really must go back to Gee and ask some questions. Suddenly Leo came quietly through the concealing greenery to find her.

'So here you are! Good grief, Nicko, this old wheel's just about had it, I'd say, wouldn't you?'

She didn't answer. He stepped closer and slid an arm around her shoulders.

'Hey, come on, snap out of it! One of your old moody moments! Aren't you going to ask what's going on? Not like you to let the grass grow under your feet.'

He swung her round, and she read the beginning of annoyance in his tanned face. Leo had never liked being left out of things. Narrowing her eyes, her anger only half-concealed, she spoke carefully.

'Oh, I know what's going on all right! You and Gee are going to upmarket this old place.

13

Isn't that what you're good at? Going to establish your reputation over here with this project, aren't you, Leo?'

His arm dropped and he frowned.

'And what's wrong with that? It's falling to bits. Can't last much longer.'

'I know. And I just want you to promise that you won't change it, but you'll never agree to that, will you? It'll be all new timber and state-of-the-art building gimmicks. Why? It won't even look like a water mill once you get to work on it!'

Leo was silent for a moment and she knew she had scored. At last he said slowly, 'Look, I know how you feel about old things, yeah, sure, I liked it, too, when we were here, goodness knows how many years ago, but things change, Nicko.'

He smiled and she watched the charm return.

'People have to change, too, you know that.'

Reaching out, he took her hand and tried to lead her away from the wheel and its stagnant pool. Nicki pulled back and ran. She heard him calling after her, but didn't care. She needed to talk to that man, Armstrong, whoever he was. And then to tell Gee just what she thought of the whole wretched idea of putting a new undignified face on this magnificent old relic.

'May I come in? I need to talk to you.'

Back at the doorway of the millhouse she

14

didn't know why she felt unsure of herself. Her daily work as an assessor of holiday accommodation enabled her to face the toughest customer, but right now she felt definitely ill at ease.

The man, a still figure in the doorway, moved back to let her enter. Nicki was thankful to see that Gee, joined now by Leo, was wandering around the outbuildings, safely out of earshot.

'I'm Nicki Bennett, Harry Bennett's daughter.'

She hoped that Dad's name, rather than Gee's, would ensure her some sort of welcome.

'Robert Armstrong. Glad to meet you, Miss Bennett.'

'Nicki, please.'

'Right, Nicki. I'm Robert.'

She liked his straightforward approach. Enjoying the smile that lit up his eyes, she took his outstretched hand and felt a tingle of delight spread through her. This man was special in some way. Quickly she snatched at her self-control. She was here on business! Suddenly she smiled at the ridiculous thought and saw Robert Armstrong's face instantly relax, as if appreciating her change of mood.

'You found the wheel?'

He was looking at her very directly, and she sensed that he saw more than just her physical form. What was it about some people, she

15

wondered abruptly, that you met them for the first time and immediately felt you'd known them for ever. Taking a deep breath, she concentrated anew.

'Yes. Like you said, it's in a bad way. But at least it's still in one piece.'

'And thank goodness for that.'

He turned from her, and looked back towards a half-open door at the far end of the passage. 'It's warmer in the workshop. Like to come in?'

At the door he waited, smiled gravely as if trying to reassure her. Nicki walked past him, her feet seeming not to touch the wooden floor.

'Your workshop?'

Stopping just inside the large, sweet-scented room, she stared around her. Littered, stained wooden benches, with rows of tools hanging above them, shone in the sunlight that filtered through big, smudgy windows. She took in the shelves, stacks of timber, a smell of paint mingling with varnish and glue, and the strange, beautiful shapes of half-finished artefacts standing in eye-catching attitudes, awaiting completion.

A small, carved bird, elegant in flight; bookshelves; half a Welsh dresser; a huge pale wooden shield, emblazoned with a complex coat of arms—so many delectable, enticing things. Delight filled her, and she swung round quickly.

16

'You're a wood-carver? A sculptor?'

'Right.'

Robert walked across the crowded room, to a small iron stove that glowed against the far wall. Crouching down, he poked at the red embers, flung on some scraps of wood, and then straightened as flames began to lick up the chimney.

'Come and get warm.'

He smiled over his shoulder, and she saw how the etched lines of his face softened. He knew about life, this man, she sensed it—pain, love and a huge awareness. Her thoughts were flying, and she was grateful when his deep voice returned her to reality.

'I think there's still some coffee left in the pot. Like one?'

'Please. And may I look? At everything?' She smiled.

'You may. But there's not much that's actually finished yet.'

He was deftly dealing with a big, old-fashioned pottery coffee-pot, his words resonating through the silent room.

'I'm working towards an exhibition, but as usual, there's not enough time, too many delays. You know how it goes, I daresay.'

'I do,' she said, recalling the work waiting for her in London.

'Well, that makes two of us in the same boat.'

There was an answering spark of

amusement in the words, and his eyes caught hers, their smiles growing more relaxed and understanding.

'Sugar with your coffee, Nicki Bennett?' he asked.

'No, thanks. Robert—'

She paused and went across the room to a particularly fine piece of blond timber propped against the wall, and stroked its smoothness.

'Yes?' he prompted her.

'The wheel.'

Turning, she saw him standing by the fire, coffee mug in one hand, clearly watching her every movement. What else did he see, she wondered sharply. Or, if not seen, what did he sense in her, for surely he was a man who read thoughts, who understood people and their hidden secrets. She pulled herself together and focused on the reason she had sought him out.

'The wheel,' she repeated. 'I miss hearing it. It was like a heart beat. That sounds fanciful.'

'No. You're absolutely right.'

He smiled, put his mug on to the table by the fire and came across the room until he stood close to her.

'Go on. Tell me more.'

She floundered for words. Embarrassment filled her, but she went on doggedly.

'I often came here as a child, when I was growing up. The wheel was a sort of engine, running the place, empowering it all.'

18

Abruptly she stopped. Why was she going on like this? Such ridiculous sentimentality! What must he think of her? But even as she left his side, ostensibly to reach for her coffee, but in fact needing to distance herself from those perceptive eyes, she found the old defiance emerging again. Looking back, she dared him to laugh at her emotional outburst.

'Stupid, aren't I?'

For a few seconds he made no reply, just stood there, still and silent in the pose that already she was beginning to recognise and enjoy. She thought momentary sadness darkened his eyes. Then he spoke quietly.

'But I couldn't have put it better myself. You're right. When the wheel stopped turning here it was as if life itself had stopped.'

Intrigued, she heard the deep voice grow almost inaudible. After a second's pause he went on slowly.

'The heart went out of the place, and of me.'

The deepening of the comfortable Devon accent, and the words themselves, touched a deep chord within her and she sensed a strange, unexpected sharing of emotions. Surprise, and then growing appreciation filled her. None of the men she had known before had ever allowed their emotions to show. This one was different. He was still looking at her, eyes shadowed now.

'You're a perceptive maid, Nicki Bennett.'

His voice lowered, and in his turn he, too, seemed to be searching for words. But she never knew what he intended to say for at that moment they heard rapid footsteps running through the room outside the workshop, and then a young teenage girl hurtled through the doorway.

'Dad, what's happening? That awful woman's here again, and some guy's wandering around with her. What're they doing? What do they want?'

Robert Armstrong crossed the space between them in three quick strides. Briefly the girl threw herself into his arms and they embraced.

'Hush, love,' he whispered, head bent low towards her.

Nicki felt an uncomfortable intruder. She put her coffee mug down hurriedly.

'Time to go,' she said brightly.

A pity, she was enjoying talking to him. She went towards the doorway, passing Robert and smiling as she added briefly, 'Thanks for the coffee and for letting me see everything.'

She was at the door as his voice recalled her.

'This is Rowan, my girl.'

He looked over her head and smiled.

'Like you, Nicki, she's a great admirer of the old wheel.'

Nicki stopped, hearing in those few words a note that intrigued her. Turning, she smiled warily down into the girl's upturned face. Children were an unknown quantity, and this one was a teenager—sure to be rebellious, outspoken, unfriendly even.

'Hi,' Rowan said, reluctantly, still encircled by her father's arm. 'Are you part of that lot, those people outside, trespassing on our land?'

'Rowan, this is Nicola Bennett. She's come to visit the old wheel. And to wish it better. Like you, she wants it to start turning again.'

The girl's sullenness died, and Nicki saw now a decidedly attractive ten or eleven-year-old, a girl with a mind of her own, she thought, her respect growing. And a daughter who clearly loved her father as deeply as he loved her. Then, in the wake of these thoughts, another emerged, quick and uncomfortable. Robert Armstrong had a daughter. Did he also have a wife? And what could it possibly matter to her if he did?

'Mr Armstrong—oh, Robert, I guess you don't mind an old woman being friendly, do you?'

Gee's flirtatious words shattered the confusion in Nicki's mind. Swinging round, she realised that her stepmother, followed by Leo, had entered the house, uninvited, and now stood in the studio doorway, beaming a persuasive smile at Robert.

'Mrs Bennett, please come in,' Robert said formally.

Nicki's heightened awareness heard the

21

barely concealed note of irritation in the quick response, and she felt instant sympathy. Really, what an intrusive nuisance Gee could be. But Robert's manners remained intact, and, leaving Rowan, he moved towards the door, inviting Gee in with a smile that showed no hint of anger.

'I apologise for this mess. But it's warm, and you're welcome.'

'Oh, my, such beautiful work.'

Gee oozed embarrassing praise as she swept the room with calculating eyes. Then she turned to look at Rowan, standing close to her father, and positively cooed. 'And is this your little girl, Robert? Hi, honey.'

Nicki flinched. She saw Robert's lips compress tightly, and then heard Rowan say indignantly, 'You know who I am! I was here when you came last time, when you said you were going to buy our home—and I'm not little. I'm practically grown-up.'

Good for you, Nicki thought, trying to hide her amusement. But I don't think you'll get away with it. She was right.

'Rowan.'

Robert's rebuke was quiet, but firm. The girl flushed, and then lowered her head. Nicki saw how she edged closer to her father, and sensed that here was a passionate and defiant personality, uncomfortable emotions and an uncomfortable age. How well she remembered!

22

As she watched, she saw Rowan lift her head again, saw the brilliant eyes narrow and brighten, and wondered if, in a minute, Gee would be told to mind her own business and go away. When Robert took charge of the awkward situation, she had an amused thought that he, too, was aware of his daughter's outspokenness.

'Mrs Bennett's welcome here, Rowan,' he chided gently. 'We're only talking about the possible sale of the mill, not actually planning it.'

And then Gee cut in sharply.

'Why, no, Robert, that's not right, and well you know it.'

Her smile had suddenly gone and she had that look about her that Nicki well recalled, of someone only trying to do the correct thing, but who was being sadly misunderstood. Then her mood changed again.

'I guess you haven't met my son, have you? All this chatter! But I see Nicki's already got to know you.'

A knowing glance was thrown in Nicki's direction and then Gee was off again.

'So rude of me not to introduce you properly!'

Over her shoulder she added, 'Leo, this is Robert Armstrong.'

Her smile returned and her voice became creamy.

'My son, Leo Forman, who runs a big

23

architectural practice in Canada and who's come over to—'

'Hi, there.'

Deftly, Leo stopped the embarrassing explanation with clipped words. He held out his hand and Robert took it. Nicki watched the two men eyeing each other, and was suddenly aware of their differing qualities. Leo was astute and ambitious, his quick mind forever concentrated on the demands of the market and his committed response to it. Robert was the creative visionary and was, she sensed, unworldly to the extent that time and money were only irritating factors in his dedication to his craft, important merely because they had the power to delay his work.

The pair had nothing in common, yet here they were, matched in their purposes of determining the future of Grealy Mill. Nicki felt terribly disturbed, but couldn't understand why. This was nothing to do with her. After all, she had only come to Devon to be with Dad, but, as she listened to what Gee was saying, her mind started to race with disbelief.

'My husband's a little unwell today, Robert,' Gee said, smiling again, her voice as innocent as a child, but Nicki saw the gleam in her bright eyes as she went on, 'And so he asked Leo and me to come and give you a message on his behalf.'

Nicki stiffened, felt anger kindle. Gee was adding lies to extravagance. What was she up

24

to?

Robert asked casually, 'And what is the message, Mrs Bennett?' and although his voice was still pleasant, Nicki heard a hint of steel underlying the words.

'Just to say he's instructed our agent to contact yours with a very good offer for the property.'

Gee sounded triumphant and Nicki suddenly hated her stepmother with the old, adolescent passion which she thought she'd grown out of but which was now renewing itself with even deeper roots.

Rowan gave a sharp cry, and stared at her father. Leo's eye caught Nicki's. It was amused, almost cocky, and as she swiftly looked back to Robert, she saw his face set into such stubborn lines that she caught her breath. This man was as difficult as his daughter.

'An offer, Robert, that you would be very unwise to refuse,' Gee finished warningly.

Those last words made Nicki abruptly realise exactly how deeply she was, indeed, involved, and not just with the mill, but with Robert Armstrong and his outspoken daughter. She felt her temper, the bane of her childish years, glow within her until it was no longer controllable. Words flew out then, strong and deeply felt.

'I don't think you're being quite straight, Gee,' she said and faced her stepmother,

25

meeting a querulous frown. 'Dad's plainly too unwell to have had any say in these arrangements you and Leo are making.'

She saw how Gee's eyes narrowed, and the thin mouth pursed, and knew she had hit the nail on the head. Encouraged, she went on.

'And even if he had, he wouldn't treat Mr Armstrong in this way.' Then a small imp of mischief made her add, 'You're behaving like a third-rate estate agent, Gee, not up to your usual standard at all.'

There was a charged silence while Gee's face grew white and grim, and Leo put his hand on Nicki's arm.

'Steady!' he said harshly. 'You don't know what you're talking about.'

'I know enough, Leo!'

She rounded on him, shaking off his hand, staring into his scowling face with hard eyes.

'And I bet there's a lot more to it, like you and Gee planning on using Dad's money. We all know how generous he is.'

From the expression on his face, she saw that her intuitive words had hit home. She was outraged.

'Well, I'm going to make sure you don't get away with it,' she snapped before swinging around, intent on leaving them to make some sort of excuse to Robert Armstrong.

She headed for the door, her mind filled with the need to return to Aunt Rachel's cottage, to tell Dad what had happened, and to

26

make sure all Gee's devious plans were wiped out before more harm could be done. Turn the mill into a transatlantic country cottage, and let Gee and Leo cheat poor old Dad out of his savings? Never!

But Gee, as always managed to have the last word.

'OK, honey, if that's how you feel,' she drawled scornfully, 'but just remember your dad's heart condition, won't you? I know you'd hate to be the one who gave him the final shock that pushed him over the edge.'

Nicki caught her breath but made no reply. Rapidly she—went out of the millhouse, thoughts churning, emotions dangerously overflowing. She knew that Robert Armstrong had made a huge impact on her, but was it only because of him that she was so determined not to see the mill misused? No, it was a whole lot of things, all mixed up. Certainly it was Robert and Rowan, but memories of Leo, too, and, suddenly, she knew it, the wheel itself.

Somehow she must get the wheel to turn again. Robert's voice echoed deep inside her— it was as if life itself had stopped—and, despite her anguish, she smiled. He felt the same as she did. Was it possible that this might bring them together?

Leaving Gee and Leo to drive home in the Land-Rover, she took the muddy footpath that crossed the fields between the mill and the cottage, desperately searching for a way of telling Dad of Gee's plotting without upsetting him.

CHAPTER TWO

Harry Bennett was on his feet in the sunlit conservatory, and Nicki's heart leaped as she saw the expression on his face. Pleasure and interest had brought out a fresh colour that gave a momentary impression of his return to good health.

'Nicki, where've you been? Gee said you'd stayed behind at the mill.'

Wondering how she was going to broach the subject of the sale of the mill, she decided to carefully edit the truth. As Gee had warned, Dad mustn't be shocked, yet somenow he must be made aware of what was going on. Playing for time, she guided him to the usual cane chair beside the French windows, and then pulled up a stool to sit beside him.

'I just felt like walking home, Dad,' she said easily. 'The footpath's muddy, but it's so lovely, coming through the fields. Did you sleep well? It's done you good. You look fine.'

Harry Bennett chuckled.

'And I feel fine. It wasn't the forty winks, though. Something much better!'

'What then?'

28

'Aunt Rachel, that's what! She phoned about twenty minutes ago. Said she's on her way down, be here in time for supper. And she's bringing a friend with her. They're booked into the pub in the village.'

'That's great, Dad. But it's a bit hard on her not to be able to stay in her own home, isn't it? I feel as if I ought to be the one who moves out.'

Harry Bennett said firmly, 'No, no, your aunt was quite decided. She and this friend, Laura someone, can't recall the surname, are happy to be at the inn. Anyway, you know Rachel and Gee don't exactly get on,' he added mischievously.

Nicki was intrigued. Clearly, Dad was immensely cheered by his sister's unexpected visit for they'd always been close.

'It'll be great to see Aunt Rachel again,' she said warmly. 'It's ages since we were all together.'

Looking at his suddenly nostalgic expression, she added curiously, 'Who's the friend, then, this Laura woman? Do we know her?'

Harry guffawed, a cheery sound she hadn't heard for a very long time.

'Most unlikely, from what Rachel said. Some feminine entrepreneur, or whatever these eccentric power-women call themselves these days!'

He grinned at Nicki.

'All rather extraordinary, actually. This Laura contacted Rachel after she'd seen her last exhibition. Rachel's doing rather well for herself, you know. Well, this Laura saw the painting of the old mill and decided there and then that she would buy it!'

'The picture?'

'No, silly, the mill!'

Harry was laughing loudly by now, and just then Gee popped her head around the doorway.

'Hey, what's up? Can I share the joke?'

Nicki caught her breath sharply. No, dear stepmother, this is one joke you definitely won't share, then relief overrode all her unkind thoughts, and she answered quickly.

'Aunt Rachel's friend is going to buy Bluebell Mill.'

Glancing around at Gee, she saw the expression of surprise grow into rising anger and couldn't resist adding wickedly, 'Good news, isn't it Gee? We all agreed that the old place needed to be restored.'

Harry cut in, plainly unaware of the tension created by her words.

'Yes, this woman's planning to turn it into a craft centre. Just what the village needs, I'd say. Get that old place working again, bring in the tourists. Can't be bad, can it? Just what I wanted to do, all those years ago. Well, sometimes things work out for the best after all, don't they?'

Gee, standing stiffly in the doorway, said in a strained voice, 'Harry, I think you've had enough excitement for the moment. Why not take a rest?'

'Rest?' Suddenly, he exploded, 'That's all my days consist of now. Rest, rest, rest.'

Leaning forward, he stared at Gee, wide-eyed and resolute.

'I tell you what, if this woman gets to work on the old mill, I'll be down there whenever I can, helping out.'

Nicki stood up. She saw the gleam in Gee's eyes, feared the damaging words that were being prepared, and tried to change the subject.

'Of course, Dad, and you must visit the wood-carver who's still working there, Robert Armstrong. He's doing some fascinating things. Now, how about a small glass of something that's good for your health and a few quiet moments while Gee and I get our gladrags on, ready for the feast!'

She bent over his chair, smoothed the wispy hair back from his forehead and smiled into his amused eyes.

'Must have you rested and at your best when Aunt Rachel arrives.'

The awkward moment was over. Nicki found the sherry bottle and left a full glass by Harry Bennett's elbow, aware that Gee still remained by the doorway. Turning, she met her stepmother's unblinking gaze. Although

31

she knew the atmosphere hadn't entirely cleared, she felt encouraged. At least the awful business of telling Dad about Gee's plans had been averted. But she could see, from Gee's pre-occupied expression, that she was already planning a new line of attack.

She was unprepared for the form it took. Gee, smiling, put a hand on her arm as she approached the door.

'Be a love and come upstairs with me, Nicki. I must wear something a bit less rural if we're going out. Give me the once over, will you, honey?'

Nicki nodded slowly. This could be just the moment for a frank talk about the mill, fraught as the idea still seemed. And yet, following Gee upstairs, she grinned to herself. It almost seemed as if fate itself was taking a hand now, in the form of this friend of Aunt Rachel's.

In the chintzy front bedroom, Gee said casually, 'Take a pew. I guess a little black dress would be too much for the local. What d'you think?'

The elegant velvet dress she pulled from the wardrobe clung to her petite figure as she smoothed it with caressing hands, bright eyes interrogating Nicki as she did so.

'You'll put all of us in the shade in that, Gee. Perhaps something a bit more, well, relaxed?'

She saw brief annoyance flit across Gee's face, watched her spin around to search in the depths of the large wardrobe and knew she must approach the problem of Aunt Rachel's friend, Laura, with great care. No scenes over supper in the pub, no taking sides. Somehow she had to keep an even balance, right in the middle of this controversial muddle.

That made her remember Leo, because he'd be on the opposite side, wouldn't he?

'You always used to look good in red, Gee,' she said placatingly. 'Haven't you got something like that now? By the way, where's Leo?'

'Gone to see a buddy somewhere. Yes, you're right—I guess this is the best bet.'

A smart red trouser suit was pulled out, inspected and finally approved. Gee tossed it on to the bed, moving across to the dressing-table where she sat down. Brushing her hair, she looked at Nicki, reflected in the mirror.

'Well, cat got your tongue, honey? We've got things to say, haven't we?' she said, unexpectedly friendly although her smile was wary.

Nicki let out the tension that had been building inside her.

'We certainly have, Gee, about the mill, and yours and Leo's plans.'

Gee said sharply, 'Not just Leo and I, honey. Your dad started it, remember, goodness knows how many years ago.'

Nicki leaned forward, engaging Gee's reflection in the mirror.

33

'But you and Leo have given Dad's idea a new lease of life, and you've changed the whole essence of it.'

She felt anger grow, heard her voice take on an edge.

'You don't want it to be a working mill at all, just a tarted-up monstrosity that will make Leo a handsome profit and give you something for your trendy friends to admire and envy!'

She came to an abrupt end, already ashamed of her lack of control. Gee smiled no longer. Her eyes, in the mirror reflection, were cloudy, and when she slowly turned around, hair brush still in her hand, Nicki was surprised at the unfamiliar expression masking the usual vivacity. Gee looked old, she thought, and felt a pang of sympathy hit her.

Looking directly into Nicki's eyes, Gee said slowly, 'You reckon I'm the wicked stepmother, don't you, as usual?'

Nicki stiffened. There was an unfamiliar note of gentle irony in the words, and for once she wasn't sure how to reply. She had anticipated fierce hostility, not this half-smiling sense of reluctant acceptance.

Carefully she replied, 'I wish you wouldn't say things like that, Gee. OK, you and I have had our ups and downs, but that was when I was younger.'

Gee's expression became wry. Turning back to the mirror, she began retouching her make up. Eyebrow pencil in hand, she said, 'Believe

34

you me, you were a real tough cookie then. Of course we had fights. But I did my best, you know, because of Harry. You and he were so darned close I felt I hardly got a look in, but, yeah, I did my best.'

Nicki thought back. She could see now just how difficult it must have been for a stepmother to take on a rebellious, and father-obsessed adolescent. And Gee was right. She had done her best. Nicki got up, stepped nearer to the dressing-table and searched for words. But Gee got there before her.

'I love your dad, Nicki, and that's the whole truth. I won't say I've always been fair to you, but I've never harmed you, or your relationship with him. And now I've brought him back, for you.'

Abruptly she threw down the lipstick she'd been applying and half-turned, staring up at Nicki, bright eyes alight with resentment.

'So don't dream up any more horrific ideas about that crazy old mill. Bluebell Mill and picnics and happy vacations were a long time ago. This is today, honey! Wake up. You're a modern gal, aren't you, career-minded, free to take your pleasure where you like? It's great for you, isn't it? Well, I suggest you just try and understand how I feel, for once.'

Nicki watched, horrified, as Gee's energy seemed to collapse, turning her into a limp, ageing figure. Gee paused, and then went on, her voice sounding lost and unhappy.

35

'Try to understand how I feel about being here,' she went on dully, 'in England, alone with a sick man, and out of my element, which, as you well know, is to be with other folks, having a good time.'

Nicki watched Gee take a deep breath, straighten her shoulders as she added slowly, 'So the mill idea was an exciting, new chapter opening up, but of course you wouldn't understand.'

Then abruptly she re-arranged her face into a brilliant smile. Preening in the mirror, she turned her head from side to side, and patted her hair.

'Well, that'll do, I guess. Don't want to overload the charm, do we?'

She flashed a wry grin at Nicki and then rose, reaching for the red jacket lying on the bed. Dressed, she gave herself a last long look in the wardrobe mirror, and then walked rapidly to the door. As she left the room, she spoke over her shoulder.

'You'll be old one day, honey. Maybe wondering how to fill the rest of your life. Just think about it. And stop making me out to be the villainess in the story.'

Nicki stood quite still in the empty room, her mind reeling. Gee's footsteps flew down the stairs, and then her voice wafted back again.

'Harry, love, are you awake? Time to go, my darling. How do I look, eh? Beautiful enough

36

to please your critical, arty sister?'

And then Harry was answering from the conservatory, quiet voice, amused and affectionate.

'You'll do, Gee. Lovely as ever. No-one could ever hold a candle to you, my sweet girl.'

Chastened and thoughtful, Nicki went to her own room to change out of her jeans and prepare for an evening which promised to be lively and hard-hitting, if nothing else.

The village inn was its usual noisily-humming self. Nicki followed Gee and Harry into the dimly-lit, low-ceilinged room and looked around her. She hadn't seen Aunt Rachel for at least three years, but there she was, browny-grey hair bunched untidily behind her ears, smiling that same devastating smile, seemingly ageless, sitting at a table beneath the far window with another, younger, woman at her side . . . the mysterious Laura.

Gee suddenly paused, pushing Harry ahead of her.

'Go on, love, you go first. You're the one she wants to see.'

She half-turned, grimaced wryly into Nicki's surprised face.

'I'm on my best behaviour, honey. Just hope Rachel recognises me.'

Nicki nodded, chuckling. So this was how Gee planned to play things, keeping Rachel sweet and pleasing poor Dad, who had always had to play pig-in-the-middle between his

37

sister and wife. A tiny feeling of admiration for Gee surfaced as she watched Dad and Aunt Rachel embrace before introductions were made. Maybe, after all, Gee wasn't as black as she'd thought.

'Nicki!' Aunt Rachel was calling her, hugging her, saying, 'Lovely to see you. It's been far too long. Now, I want you to meet Laura Humphries, my new patron. Laura, this is my beautiful and talented niece, Nicola.'

Nicki flushed slightly.

'Come on, Aunt Rachel,' she said quickly, 'that's a bit over the top.'

She looked at Laura Humphries.

'Hi,' she said casually. 'I'm only moderately clever, and certainly not beautiful. And please, call me Nicki.'

Rachel's laughing comment went unheard. Laura Humphries held out her hand, and Nicki looked into coolly calculating, wide-spaced hazel eyes as she shook it. A cold hand, instantly withdrawn, she thought it matched the expression of restraint that filled Laura's intelligent and sophisticated face. Nicki felt immediate antipathy stir.

So this was one of the power-women Dad joked about but she was intuitively certain that Laura was not one who had ever joked. Life to Laura, Nicki guessed, was serious and ambitious. Abruptly, she hoped it also held integrity. How terrible if the scheme of restoring poor old Bluebell Mill never came to fruition.

Intent on building bridges, she said carefully, 'Welcome to the Bennett family, Laura. We're all delighted that you could come down with Aunt Rachel.'

And then, receiving a dismissive nod of the expensively honey-streaked head, she turned back to Harry who was collecting orders for drinks.

'Let me help, Dad. I'll carry the tray.'

She was thankful to be at the bar, away from the already charged atmosphere at the crowded table, leaving Aunt Rachel to question Gee about Dad and explain circumstances to Laura. Soon, she knew, the question of the sale of the mill would come up, and she wondered how Gee, despite her promise to behave, would react when she finally realised her plan was being destroyed. And then she thought of Leo. He should be here, surely, to support his mother.

As if she had conjured him up, suddenly she heard his voice. Looking along the length of the curving mahogany bar, she saw him, sitting at the far end, a tankard of beer in front of him, chatting to a man standing at his side.

Robert Armstrong! Nicki wondered at the surge of excitement that spurted through her, and told herself not to be such a fool. Gee thought her modern and liberated, yet this uncontrolled spasm of delight hinted at old-fashioned romanticism, hardly appropriate to a business woman! But then, perhaps she wasn't quite the trendy woman she imagined herself to be.

A smile curved her set lips then, and without knowing it, she let it grow as she looked at the tall, dark-haired man talking so intently to Leo. And then he glanced up and their eyes met, and his own smile matched hers in a way that made her whole body glow with enjoyment. Forgetting everything else, she moved away from the tray of drinks collecting on the bar beside her, and went towards him.

'Nicki, can I get you a drink?' he asked as she drew nearer.

She smiled, hearing in the polite words an irresistible undercurrent.

'No thanks, Robert. Dad's getting me one.'

She paused, dragging her eyes away from his, for Leo was beside them. She felt him watching, calculating. Disarmingly she turned towards him.

'Thought you were off to see a buddy?'

His answering smile was tight and expressionless, but she sensed his understanding of her heightened feelings.

'Ma's been talking, has she? Well, this was the buddy, but of course you know each other already.'

Nicki caught Robert's eye and then quickly looked back at Leo.

'And you've been discussing this latest development about the mill?' she asked warily.

40

'You both know about this woman, Laura Humphries, planning to restore it into a craft centre?'

The moment the words were said she knew she'd been stupid to bring it all into the open, for Leo was looking at her with the cold, hostile expression that she remembered of old. In those days, she had done all she could to avoid angering him.

Now she knew, with fierce pride, that she had lost all that fear long ago. If he was going to make things unpleasant, then she could well retaliate. And so she lifted her head a little higher, challenging him with her steady gaze, and waiting silently for his reply.

'Don't count your chickens till they're hatched, Nicki,' he chided lightly. 'Remember that Mom and I have made an equally good offer.'

'What nonsense!' she snapped back. 'You had no plans at all to restore it. What you had in mind was a trendy sort of conference house, or holiday flats or . . . '

'Calm down, sweetie.'

She froze. Leo's charm had abruptly returned, and he was smiling at her with what seemed easy affection. While she was considering how to cope with such a deceitful ploy, Robert's deep voice cut in.

'Look, the last thing I want is to cause unpleasantness between you.'

Putting down his tankard, he looked at her.

41

His eyes were shadowed and she sensed his displeasure at the awkward scene being played out so blatantly in front of him. But it was vital that he should know how things were between Leo and herself.

'Please, don't worry about me being rude to Leo. He's quite used to it,' she said, and then couldn't stop herself adding firmly, 'We're not involved with each other, you know.'

'What?'

Leo made a grab for her hand, his smile warm and amused. He glanced at Robert and grinned broadly.

'She loves to play hard to get!'

Nicki felt her fury grow. She pulled herself free from Leo's grasp and turned towards Robert, aware that she was only making matters worse, but not caring.

'Don't believe him! He's just playing games, as usual.'

She thought she saw the shadows retreat from Robert's eyes and was exhilarated. Spontaneously, she added, 'Why don't you come over and meet Laura Humphries? She's here with Aunt Rachel. I'm sure she'd like to see you.'

Robert paused, and she recognised brief indecision on his face.

'But we've already planned a meeting for tomorrow morning.'

Then his expression cleared and she thought again how honest and sincere he

42

seemed.

'It's sensible to hit when the iron's hot though, isn't it?' he added. 'OK, Nicki, I'd like to meet her.' His smile warmed her. 'Thanks for your help.'

Delighted, she led the way through the crowded room, uncaringly aware that Leo's frown, as he followed, was set in increasingly angry lines, but the knowledge did nothing to dent her new-found happiness. Leo was of no importance. Only Robert, and the mill, were.

'Aunt Rachel, this is Robert Armstrong who lives at Grealy Mill. He's a sculptor, a wood carver.'

She watched with pleasure as Robert's easy charm instantly converted Aunt Rachel to his side in the tug-of-war to come. And Aunt Rachel would be a worthy opponent, as she knew well. For years she had kept Gee and Leo at arm's length, plainly acknowledging them only as relatives who must be tolerated, but not loved.

Nicki went round the table, introducing Dad, whose patient smile supported her own feelings, and then Laura, sitting straight in her chair, elegantly-painted figures idly holding a glass of sparkling water.

'Laura, this is Robert Armstrong, owner of the mill, who works as a—'

She got no further. Abruptly, Laura's smile grew far from politically correct as she raised one delicate eyebrow and said warmly, 'But of course I know you, Robert! In fact, I've had it in mind for ages to look you up. The sculpture you did of Lord Exton's coat of arms really appealed to me.'

The smile was captivating, and the beautiful eyes thawed into surprising friendliness. Nicki felt her heart race. She'd realised Robert's work was good, of course, but Laura actually knew and admired it! Then coldness swept through her. This terrifyingly sophisticated art-lover appeared to be throwing herself at Robert, while she herself knew nothing of art. So how could she hope to meet Robert, or cope with Laura, on equal terms?

Numbly, Nicki watched Robert's answering expression of recognition, heard his voice grow bright with pleasure.

'Of course! Last winter in Birmingham, wasn't it? Yes, I do remember!'

Still smiling at Robert, Laura leaned back in her chair as the two men seated themselves. Leo drew Nicki down beside him, leaving Robert to sit between Gee and Harry, who moved up to make room. Nicki was increasingly furious with herself. She hadn't expected anything like this when she suggested introducing Robert. But then, how could she possibly have known that Laura had an ulterior motive in wanting to buy the mill? She must have known who owned it!

A small niggle of near-hatred centred deep within Nicki. So Robert was the real prize, was he? Her lips pursed. Well, she just might have something to say that would change circumstances to her own advantage. All's fair in love and business, isn't it? Then she frowned with exasperation. All her experience with difficult clients had not, as yet, fitted her for the role of manipulator in a fight with another woman, it seemed.

Laura was talking again.

'I've got a wonderful sponsor. He's entirely committed to restorations and the setting up of centres for the crafts. He's a great admirer of William Morris.'

Nicki watched Robert's smile broaden. She had the hateful feeling that he and Laura were really good friends, as he said warmly, 'Everything beautifully hand-made, for the use of the common man! I certainly agree with that idea.'

'And your work particularly interested him.'

Nicki glowered. She had the feeling that patron and craftsman were forging a relationship that she could never hope to share. She knew nothing about William Morris except that he was a craftsman who specialised in making useful and beautiful artefacts.

It was this very helpless feeling that made her chip in then, with a bright force that caught everyone's attention, sending a little quiver around the table.

'This all sounds terribly precious and over my head! Can't we get down to the nitty-gritty instead? What really matters, surely, Laura, is that you're going to chat up this sponsor so that he buys the mill. And then you can organise the restoration, which is what's so vital.'

She stopped abruptly. All eyes were on her. Aunt Rachel looked surprised but slightly amused, while Dad was plainly shocked at her outburst. She saw that Gee was outraged, bright eyes narrowed and hard. And Leo? She could feel his hostility reaching out towards her. She slid another inch back in her chair. Fixing her gaze on Laura's perfectly composed face Nicki added shortly, and with clear-cut hostility, 'Well, aren't you?'

Just for a moment, no-one spoke. She felt the atmosphere grow tense and disliked what she was doing, but then reassured herself—after all, someone had to sort out this muddle, otherwise they'd be here all night with no decision made, and Gee would go on and on.

It was Laura and Gee who answered together, their words clashing.

'My sponsor is firmly committed to the purchase.'

'But Leo and I are buying, you know that, Nicki.'

And then Robert's deep voice cut into the shocked moment of ensuing silence.

'I'm sorry, Mrs Bennett, but Mrs Humphries and I are meeting tomorrow morning to discuss her sponsor's offer.'

Nicki sucked in a deep breath of relief and looked at him, expecting to see triumphant decision on his face, but to her surprise he was expressionless. When, abruptly, he half-turned and met her gaze she was shocked to see how disturbed he actually was. The pale blue eyes had become as cold as icebergs and involuntarily she gasped. Before she could offer him an apology, for she imagined he was angry with her for interfering, Gee was talking again, her voice shriller than usual, clear words loud enough to make the other people in the bar turn to look towards the table.

'Why, this is preposterous, Robert! My offer was made in good faith that you were keen to sell, and we've suggested a price well over the value of the wretched place.'

She glared across at Robert who met her eyes, but remained expressionless.

'How dare you throw me off like this!' she went on, words fast and forceful. 'Oh, but of course! I understand.'

Nicki watched her stepmother's face patch with colour, saw how her thin mouth grew tight and unattractive, as she added furiously, 'You and Mrs Humphries are old friends, if that's the right way to describe your relationship.'

'Steady, old girl,' Harry remonstrated, his hand on her arm.

Gee ignored him and shook herself free.

'So naturally you'll take her offer before

mine.'

'Before our offer, Mother.'

Leo's voice was strong and Nicki had a sudden grateful feeling of reprieve. She was hating every second of this ghastly scene, even though she herself had started it. Gee, she knew from the past, could carry on in the same unpleasant vein for ages, so surely it was the lesser of two evils that Leo had decided to take over.

Beside her, he nonchalantly linked his hands on the table, looking around the circle of faces that watched him so intently.

'No need to get quite so exercised, Mom,' he drawled. 'Have a sip of your drink and calm down a bit.'

His light voice was amused and quiet. Gee's eyes flashed a warning, but she said no more, and when Harry smiled at her, she merely picked up her glass and jerked herself away from him.

Leo looked across at Robert and went on affably.

'My mother is naturally disappointed, and who can blame her? After all, buying the old mill and restoring it has been Harry's dream for many years, which is the reason we made our offer.'

Nicki slid a glance at her father. He nodded in agreement, but frowned slightly, and she guessed that she'd been right in surmising that Gee and Leo hadn't told him of their own

48

scheme for Bluebell Mill.

'But there, it seems we'll just have to find another old, run-down ruin, won't we?'

Leo's smile was casual, yet cold enough to freeze anyone into submission, Nicki thought, recognising a ploy used frequently in their shared growing-up. Make your victim think he's got off lightly before you apply the thumb-screws. She shivered and was thankful when Robert got to his feet, glancing at his watch before looking around the table.

'I really must go,' he said. 'I don't want to leave Rowan alone any longer, but can I get anyone another drink first?'

It was Aunt Rachel who returned the situation to normality, answering cheerfully, 'Kind of you, Mr Armstrong, but we're planning to eat.' She swept a determinedly warm smile around her sparring family. 'I don't know about you all, but Laura and I are starving. Haven't had a bite since lunchtime!'

Her cheeriness brought a few wan smiles to faces, and then Harry's hand closed over hers.

'Well said, my dear! Never declare war on an empty stomach!'

He winked comically at Nicki before turning to Gee, and adding, 'Remember how good the steak-and-kidney pie used to be? Shall we make it two, my darling?'

The atmosphere relaxed. Laura and Leo, aided by Aunt Rachel, scanned the menu, while Gee muttered acidly that Harry mustn't be disappointed if the food wasn't as wonderful as he remembered it. Things changed, didn't he realise that?

Nicki was very aware of Robert standing opposite, clearly a little hesitant about leaving, listening, watching, plainly intent on discovering more about everybody. When, eventually, his eyes rested on her, she smiled encouragingly. Knowing him to be a passionate man, she hadn't been able to reconcile his bland expression when listening to Gee's hurtful tirade. Yet she sensed that he understood more than he showed outwardly.

This reminded her of her own volatile temperament, and for a second, guilt tugged at her mind. She really must control herself in future. No more outbursts, no more bickering with Leo. Then she was back to watching Robert, and wondering, would he stay and share a meal with them? Would he make a point of talking to Laura, if he did? And also, and much more important—would he forgive her for throwing the stone into the pond and raising such difficult, storm-swept ripples?

Then, even as he turned to smile at her, and opened his mouth to speak, his attention was arrested by the barman calling his name.

'Robert Armstrong? Phone call for you. Your daughter, I think.'

Nicki saw the expression on Robert's face change swiftly as he instantly went towards the phone. Uneasy at the thought of meeting

50

Gee's querulous eyes across the table, she moved slowly to the bar, joining Harry and Leo, who were ordering the meals. Leo glanced round, grinning wickedly, as he made room for her beside them.

'Quite the little terrorist, aren't you, Nicko? Plant a bomb, and then see what happens! Well, I've got news for you, sweetie.' His grin died. 'Dynamite does more damage than you could ever guess. And it often sets off another explosion somewhere else, in retaliation.'

He stopped short, bending to listen to Harry, and answering briefly, 'That's it, scampi and salad for Mom and chilli for me.'

Then he turned his attention back to Nicki, handing her a glass of white wine and saying, 'Try this, and remember that explosions tend to get increasingly dangerous.'

His eyes caught hers and she saw how cold they were, despite his seemingly humorous tone of voice.

'I just hope you know what you've set in motion, darling girl.'

But Nicki hardly heard the last words. At the side of the room, Robert replaced the telephone and stood for a moment as if uncertain what to do next. Nicki saw his face, stern and set, and without even thinking what she was doing, put down her glass and went to his side.

'What is it, Robert? Something wrong?'

He swung round, his eyes resting on her and

51

an expression of decision suddenly lighting up his face.

'Nicki! Yes, I've got to get back to the mill in a hurry. Someone's trying to break in, from what Rowan said. But I haven't got my car. Your friend, Leo, picked me up.'

He eyed her with a wry, apologetic smile and she understood at once.

'Of course! Mine's outside. I'll have you there in no time.'

Without bothering to explain to the family, and certainly not to Leo, who watched, from the bar, with a look of definite hostility, Nicki led the way to her car in the carpark. She drove fast and expertly, feeling tension mount in the man beside her. As they approached the mill, she found herself praying that Rowan was safe and that no harm had been done to the old building. She also hoped Robert was perhaps glad that it was she who was here, beside him, and not that odious Laura Humphries!

CHAPTER THREE

Robert shot out of the car before Nicki braked. She watched him run to the millhouse door, find a key and open it. And then Rowan appeared, flying into his arms, face crumpled and tear-stained.

52

Nicki's emotions flared. She didn't care now whether Robert wanted her here or not. She was on the spot and she would do all she could to help him and Rowan.

'I'll look after Rowan. Go and phone the police,' she said quickly.

'Thanks,' he said shortly, persuading Rowan to leave the shelter of his arms. 'Give her a drink, will you? There's orange in the fridge.' He lowered his voice to a murmur. 'And let her talk.'

And then, before either Rowan or Nicki could say anything more, he disappeared into the gloom of the millhouse. Nick's thoughts floundered as she hugged Rowan to her. Robert was strong, powerfully built, and quite capable of tackling an intruder, but what if a gun was pulled on him? She shut her eyes, quickly banishing the awful images. She smiled determinedly into Rowan's unhappy eyes.

'Let's do as your dad says. A drink to recoup our spirits! And then tell me what happened.'

Sitting Rowan near the Aga, she bent to open the fridge as Robert returned from his tour of the building, saying shortly, 'Nothing to worry about. Just a stone through the window. I'll put up some boarding. Could you stay, Nicki? I don't want to leave Rowan alone.'

'Of course,' she said warmly. 'Rowan's going to tell me what happened.'

Robert shot her a smile as he collected some tools before setting out to cover the broken window.

'I'm grateful,' was all he said, but the tone of his voice spoke more than the two words.

'OK then,' Nicki said encouragingly to Rowan, hunched in her chair and ignoring the offered can of juice. 'Let's pretend I'm the village constable and you're the lady of the manor.'

There was a small pause. Rowan slowly reached for the can and opened it thoughtfully, eyes downcast.

'Come along, madam, don't keep the law waiting, if you please.'

The jokey voice was gruff and Nicki twisted her face into a disapproving grimace, wondering just how long she could keep this up. Suddenly, with great relief, she saw Rowan's bleak expression dissolve into a weak grin.

'Well, actually, constable, I've just found a body in the library.'

Now Rowan was laughing as she put the can to her mouth. Nicki felt satisfaction spread through her. Resuming her comic disguise, she went on, 'Oh, yes? And at exactly what time did you find this body, ma'am? And did you by any chance know him or her?'

She pulled out an imaginary notebook, sucked the tip of an invisible pencil, and grinned persuasively at Rowan.

'It was the end of EastEnders,' Rowan said promptly, looking serious again. 'Mrs Jones
54

had just come to take Gemma home. We often watch telly together if Dad has to go out. He said he wouldn't be long, so after Gemma had gone I expected him home soon. But he didn't come, and I was wondering if I ought to ring up Mrs Jones again and tell her I was alone, when—'

'Take your time, Rowan. It's all over. You're quite safe.'

The girl nodded.

'Thank goodness Dad's back. I was really scared. I heard someone outside, and when I looked through the window I saw, well, a sort of shadowy figure. A man, I suppose.'

She bowed her head, putting her arms around her body and hugging herself.

'And then the stone came through the window. I stepped back. None of the glass hit me but—but—I was frightened.'

Tears welled up, and quickly Nicki kneeled beside her, arms around the shaking shoulders.

'Of course you were. I would have been petrified.'

Rowan slid a doubtful glance sideways.

'Would you?'

'Honestly,' Nicki said stoutly. 'I think you were incredibly brave.'

'Actually,' Robert's voice said from the doorway, 'I have a fairly good notion of who it was.'

Coming into the room, he crossed to the dresser and put down the hammer he carried.

'A troublesome old man called Archie Luscombe, if I'm not wrong. We've had problems with him before.'

Nicki quailed at the expression on his face. She had thought Leo a force to be reckoned with, but now Robert appeared ten times more menacing and authoritative. And she understood why. Anyone who threatened either his beloved daughter or his property should think twice before repeating the offence. She was glad when he looked at Rowan, and she saw all the hardness disappear.

'Remember how the old rogue came and told us we had no right to fence that bit of scrub beyond the wheel?' he asked, and as Rowan nodded, he went on, 'I only fenced it because I didn't want him or his cat falling into the wheelpit. But he said it was his boundary, one of those unresolved problems over the years, I suppose, and he wanted it kept free.'

Rowan smiled up at him, and Nicki saw relief chase the tension from her face.

'Was it him who threw the stone, then?'

'I daresay.' Robert nodded, his voice gentle. 'I'll have a word with him in the morning. Now, what about bedtime? Go and have your bath, and Nicki and I will rustle up some supper and we'll have it together down here. All right, my girl?'

Rowan got to her feet, and leaned against him, smiling. He kissed her brow before

56

turning her towards the door.

'All safe,' he said quietly. 'Nothing to be afraid of. Off you go.'

She went without a backward glance and Nicki heard her footsteps going up the stairs. She looked at Robert.

'Are you sure it was that old man? Nothing worse?'

Robert stood in front of the Aga and was silent for a moment.

'No, I'm not sure,' he said at last. 'Can't be, because I wasn't here. But it's possible it was Archie.'

His expression became grim and Nicki held her breath, glad when he relaxed, smiling at her with wry amusement.

'Sorry,' he said, with a twist of his lips. 'We Celts get awfully caught up with our enemies, you know! But I'll try and make up for it by giving you a good supper. Would you settle for scrambled eggs and smoked salmon?'

Nicki returned the smile.

'Would I not! But where's such a delicacy coming from at this hour of the night?'

'The freezer, of course.'

He was his familiar, charming self again, no trace of the hard expression that had threatened a few minutes before. Nicki felt comfortably reassured, and at once got to grips with the freezer.

'Good girl,' he said lightly, turning to the sink to wash his hands. 'Eggs in the basin on the dresser, butter in the fridge. You know what, Nicki Bennett? You and I make a good team. Don't you think?'

Nicki made no answer, but her inner thoughts agreed fervently. A far better team, she hoped, than Robert and Laura Humphries had ever made in the past, or would make again.

The scrambled eggs were delicious, and so was the company of Rowan and her father. Nicki felt relaxed and indulged. All her fears about Laura had disappeared, and she even hoped that he might, another time, ask her out for a drink, or perhaps suggest a cup of coffee in his studio.

Rowan was reluctant to go to bed, when Robert looked at the clock, before raising an eyebrow in her direction.

'But I like being here, talking to Nicki,' she said, deliberately assuming a little-girl pout.

'It's far too late, my girl. You'll never be up in the morning.'

But Robert's reply sounded to Nicki like that of the definitive, indulgent father. She sensed that Rowan could wrap him around her little finger without any difficulty, and had to hide her smile when Robert frowned, even as he nodded resignedly.

'Another half-hour, then.'

Rowan giggled, looking at her father with such affection and trust that Nicki almost envied him. To be loved like that—she bowed

58

her head for a moment to hide the vulnerable expression that she knew lit her face. She liked Robert a lot, but she wasn't ready, yet, to let him into her inner thoughts.

Rowan wriggled in her chair, playing with the ties of her bathrobe, her self-congratulatory expression suddenly darkening.

'That Mr Luscombe, will he do it again? Throw stones?'

Nicki heard the note of concern, and was glad when Robert made nothing of the question.

'Of course not,' he said casually. 'He's probably been at the cider pot and remembered how he tripped over the wire last week. I'll see him tomorrow, sort it all out. We'll be friends in the end, you'll see.'

'Mmm. Hope so. He's a nice old man. A bit funny, I suppose, but he talks about the old days when this was a proper mill. It's great. Dad, you won't sell to that crazy old woman, will you? The one who talks all the time. American, is she?'

Nicki heard herself chip in, 'Canadian, actually.'

'Oh!' Rowan was plainly embarrassed. 'Sorry. Didn't mean to be rude.'

'It's OK, Rowan. Gee's my stepmother and yes, she is a bit crazy, at times. And, no, I don't imagine your dad will sell the mill to her.'

She stopped short, glancing up at him, receiving the smallest nod, and then went on, reassured.

'Actually, he's had a better offer, from another woman.'

He was still looking at her and she felt her colour rise, but went on steadily.

'Someone in the art world, Laura Humphries, who's made a much better suggestion.'

Rowan frowned.

'But that means he's still going to sell.'

Robert took over.

'But, love, we'll go on living here, and working. The idea, you see, is to restore the mill and make a craft centre out of it.'

His musical voice was unemotional, but Nicki was beginning to know him now. He had depths which he chose not to reveal. And this was one of them. She recognised the intent expression in his light eyes, the straight, still posture that made almost a sculpture out of him. She knew that Laura's plan for the mill was dear to his heart, and that he would do all he could to bring the old building back into use. Suddenly she was unable to keep quiet as the importance of that thought took form.

'So, the wheel will turn again?' she asked.

A moment's silence, while both Rowan and Robert looked at her, then at each other, before Robert said slowly, with the smallest tremor in his low voice, 'The wheel will turn, which is what we all want, isn't it, Rowan?'

Rowan nodded. Nicki saw the vivid eyes

swim, and wondered why, until Rowan said, in an unsteady voice. 'Like it did, when Mum was here. Wasn't it funny, though, how the wheel broke down the very day she left? As if it was as unhappy as we were.'

Nicki glanced anxiously at Robert. His eyes were on Rowan. He leaned forward, laid his hands over hers and smiled determinedly.

'Yes, my lovely girl, you're right. But that was yesterday, and now it's today. And we're looking forward to tomorrow, aren't we?'

Rowan nodded, set her lips, and smiled back at him. And Nicki, watching, suddenly understood Robert's earlier words. What had he said? When the wheel stopped turning it was as if life itself had stopped. With his wife leaving him, it must have seemed just like that. How agonising life could be.

Robert's voice intruded into her thoughts, his voice resolutely cheerful, even slightly amused.

'So we must all think about the wheel turning again, keep it in our minds, make it happen.'

His eyes sought Nicki's and she saw they were dark with concealed emotion

'There's power for you!' he said, a brief smile blazing out. 'A good old Celtic charm! Never known it fail.'

Then, his voice growing more gentle, he returned to the problems of parenthood.

'Now, no more arguments, child! Bed!'

Rowan laughed, and the spell was broken.

' 'Night, Nicki,' she said, her eyes warm and friendly. 'See you again soon. 'Night, Dad.'

She was just about to go upstairs, when there was a loud banging at the front door.

'OK,' Robert said reassuringly, 'I'll go. And if it's Archie I'll tell him to come back in the morning. We don't want any more alarms and excursions tonight, thanks very much.'

But it wasn't the cross old neighbour who came into the kitchen at Robert's brusque invitation. It was Leo Forman, and he had an expression on his face that made Nicki instantly get to her feet.

'Sorry to intrude,' he said smoothly, eyes intimating what the words did not quite convey, 'but I've come to fetch Nicki home. It's her dad.'

'Oh, no! Not another heart attack!'

Nicki tensed, guilt immediately suggesting that she should never have left him.

'Hard to say. Ma's looking after him.'

Leo's all-seeing eyes turned from Nicki to Rowan and then to Robert.

'What a shame,' he went on blandly, 'upsetting this comfy little tête-à-tête. But I knew Nicki'd want to get home at once.'

Robert's face was set.

'You could have phoned.'

'Guess I could,' Leo drawled, 'but here I am, instead. Coming, then, Nicko?'

Turning, he walked to the door and she

followed quickly, thoughts only of Dad and his need of her. She smiled apologetically at Rowan, then felt Robert's eyes on her. She looked back at him.

'I'm sorry,' she said simply, hearing the anxiety in her voice, and praying that he would understand.

He nodded but said nothing. As she stepped out of the house into the quiet night, she glanced round, hoping he would smile, say something she could carry home with her as a hope of some sort. But, with Rowan beside him in the doorway, he merely asked Nicki to give Mr Bennett his best wishes, and then watched her get into her car as Leo climbed into the Land-Rover, just ahead of her in the deserted carpark. The door shut, and Nicki prepared to follow Leo back to Rose Cottage.

She was so busy thinking about Dad that she automatically switched off the engine as Leo left the Land-Rover and came back to her window.

'What is it?'

Unprepared, she cried out as he wrenched open the door and roughly pulled her from the car.

'Leo! What on earth?'

'Come here.'

His voice was unexpectedly loud, and she sensed his determination, but to do what? Her anger rose, driving out her fears about Dad. As he put his arms around her she struggled.

'Stop it! I don't know what you're playing at, but let me go! I've got to get home.'

'Not yet, sweetie,' he said and again his voice was unnecessarily loud in the hushed evening.

A frisson of fear stabbed her. What was this unpleasant little scene about?

'All in good time, Nicko mine.'

This time Leo was almost shouting, and abruptly she realised the name of the game, for the millhouse door was creaking open, and they were caught in the light streaming out into the dark carpark.

Ashamed and furious, she heard Robert's deep voice saying, 'Nicki? Anything wrong?'

But before she could answer, Leo pulled her closer, shouting back over her shoulder, in a voice full of mockery, 'Nothing to concern you, Armstrong. Get back to your cosy fire. We're making our own bit of warmth out here!'

There was a moment's silence and Nicki's fury grew, imagining what Robert, and Rowan, must be thinking. Then she heard footsteps crunching over the flagstones. With a surge of extra strength she pushed Leo away from her and swung round to meet Robert's hard-set face. He held out her shoulder bag, saying politely, but in a voice that chilled her blood, 'A good thing you're still here. You left this.'

She felt breathless and defeated. It seemed that Leo's devilish plan had succeeded, if Robert's bitter expression was anything to go by. But she was angry, too, and refused to give in. She snatched the bag from his hand, dumped it into the car and said rapidly, as she climbed in after it, 'Don't believe all you see, Robert, and never believe a word Leo tells you.'

Then she pulled out, missing the Land-Rover by an inch, and roared away down the lane, intent on putting the hateful incident behind her.

Gee was halfway up the stairs as Nicki came through the front door. Jokily, she said, 'Hey, what's up? Someone chasing you?'

'Where's Dad? How is he?'

Nicki ran up the stairs, following Gee on to the small landing. Gee scowled, lifting an elegant finger.

'Sh! He was probably fast asleep until you raised all this rumpus.'

Nicki stared into her stepmother's reproving eyes. 'He's OK?'

'Haven't I just told you?'

Nicki drew in a long, deep breath and leaned against the banisters.

'But Leo said . . . '

Wearily then she shook her head.

'I see. Sorry, Gee. I got something wrong, that's all.'

How could she tell Gee what her beloved son had been up to? She turned away, her heartbeat settling into a more comfortable rhythm, knowing that she would never forgive

65

Leo for playing such a vile trick on her. Before she reached the hallway, Gee's half-whisper floated down the stairs, and she glanced up again.

'Harry's fine, honey. Enjoyed his evening. Even started counting his chickens over this dreary old Grealy Mill business. Even though we can't buy it after all, looks like he still wants a hand in the restoration.'

A mischievous smile sharpened her face.

'Guess that Laura Humphries woman knows how to charm a guy!'

Nicki nodded silently. Yes, Laura certainly charmed the guys—Dad and Robert included. And now, after seeing her in Leo's embrace, Robert would probably turn to Laura and their old friendship.

Gee yawned.

'I'm exhausted!'

Her voice took on an edge.

'Be on your way back to London tomorrow, won't you, honey? Well, you can forget our plan for the old place. Leo's still keen on it, but I've given up. Too much hassle. Seems that Robert Armstrong thinks he can do much better with Laura. G'night, then, honey.'

A door closed and the house was quiet. Dad was OK! Nicki went into the kitchen and made strong black coffee, thoughts too busy, too hot with fury, to contemplate sleep. Leo had made a fool of her. Robert must think she was a tart, and Rowan—what effect would that wretched

66

scene have made on her adolescent mind?

But Gee had given up all thoughts of modernising the mill, and surely Leo would, too, once he'd thought it all over. Yet she recalled his youthful persistence, and felt uneasy, remembering. But Dad was OK. Be glad about that! Forget everything else. Alone in the unlit, shadowy conservatory, staring out into the moon-touched garden, Nicki told herself over and again that she must be thankful for that one, small, all-important mercy. And, as her mind relaxed, she knew that she was.

The next day she made plans to leave directly after lunch, telling herself not to think about Leo or Robert, not even the mill itself. But she still found herself wondering when Laura was meeting Robert, and, despite her resolution not to, couldn't help imagining that meeting. She jerked herself back into the present. She must concentrate on avoiding Leo, who was mooching around the garden in a filthy temper, eyeing her menacingly. Why not take Dad out for a drive? No, not to the mill, she couldn't bear that. And later she would help Gee with the lunch dishes before leaving.

But it didn't work out like that. She had taken Dad to Sandy Beach where she had parked just behind the dunes, looking out at the blue-green ocean curling around the scallop-shaped cove.

'Remember the fun we had here, Nicki?' Dad had asked, and she had thought back with pleasurable nostalgia. 'Beach cricket, picnics, swimming, happy days!'

The vivid memories had kept them busy during the drive home. And then, as Nicki helped Dad into his usual chair in the conservatory, Gee called from the kitchen.

'Someone to see you, Nicki. OK, honey, go right through.'

Nicki saw Rowan standing awkwardly in the doorway.

'Hello,' she said brightly. 'Just in time to have a drink with us! Dad, this is Robert's daughter, Rowan. Rowan, this is my dad, Harry Bennett.'

'Hi, Mr Bennett.'

Rowan held out a polite hand. Harry shook it with a warm smile.

'Sit down, young lady, while Nicki gets us a drink. What about a nice herb tea? My sister, whose cottage this is, is a great herbalist. She grows the lot out there.'

He gestured towards the garden, and Nicki, halfway to the kitchen, heard Rowan's answering voice grow relaxed and easy, as she said, 'Can I go out and look? Dad and I grow mint, for mint sauce, you know, and sometimes as a drink.'

When Nicki came back to the conservatory, she found Rowan and Dad chatting about old wives' tales and herbal remedies.

'Onions are good for sore throats,' Rowan told Harry very seriously. 'Next time you get one, try an onion.'

Nicki sat and listened. Seeing Rowan here, she felt a small part of the burden on her shoulders lift. Obviously Rowan was unconcerned about seeing her in Leo's arms last night. Nicki's smile broadened. And then, as the conversation paused, she said lightly, 'Lovely to see you. Just out for a walk, are you?'

Rowan turned.

'No,' she said. 'I've come 'specially.'

Nicki caught her breath. Could she have a message from Robert?

'I just wanted to get away from the mill,' she said pouting childishly. 'That Mrs Humphries and Dad are talking business all the time. So I came here, to see you.'

Nicki's disappointment eased. Thank goodness the child regarded her as an ally! She longed to ask what was happening at the mill, whether the vital decision to sell to Laura's sponsor had been taken, but of course it would be wrong to question Rowan about it. And then a fresh worry stabbed. If Robert accepted Laura's offer, her own tenuous link with him must necessarily end. There would be no visiting the mill any more.

Just as she was trying to banish these thoughts, Leo appeared at the French window, staring in at them. Nicki tensed. They had said nothing to each other since that angry parting last night, and she feared he might be going to renew his attack. But, as she met his eyes, she realised he was planning something new. And that plan appeared to focus on Rowan.

'Hi, there,' he said, with a friendly grin, folding himself into the chair next to Rowan. 'Have we got news of the mill, then? Hey, you're in the fashion, aren't you, with that red mop of hair? Red's in these days, you know!'

He reached out a hand and touched the shining curls that fell over her shoulder. Rowan flinched, scowled at him, and then deliberately looked towards Nicki, ignoring the admiring glance Leo was giving her.

'Actually, I came to tell you something, Nicki,' Rowan said purposefully.

Such poise in a ten-year-old, Nicki thought wryly, seeing Leo's quick frown as he realised he was being ignored.

'I knew you'd want to know,' Rowan went on. 'Dad saw Mr Luscombe this morning, the old guy who lives next door to us, the one who threw the stone through the window last night. And Dad told him there's no need to get so uptight about his old boundary.'

Leo chipped in breezily.

'Not trouble at t'mill, I hope?'

Rowan gave him a scornful glance before looking back at Nicki.

'He's not real trouble. Dad's persuaded him that it's safer to have a boundary fence, but

70

that he needn't think of it as a real boundary, if you see what I mean!'

Nicki and Harry laughed, but Leo's expression grew sharp. Nicki felt apprehensive. How well she knew his devious ways. She wished he would leave them alone without any more teasing or facetious remarks. She decided to give him a kick-start. Standing up, she collected the empty glasses, and said to Dad, 'I'll take Rowan home before lunch. Anything you want before we go?'

Harry gave Rowan a big smile.

'Nothing, thanks, love. And you, young lady, be sure to come and see me again. I've got a book about herbs you can borrow.'

Rowan, on her feet, returned the smile.

'I'd like that, Mr Bennett. One afternoon after school, thanks.'

She followed Nicki out of the conservatory without looking at Leo, whose expressionless eyes trailed her in silence. But it was Leo who left first, while Nicki and Rowan said goodbye to Gee. As they went out of the garden towards the parked car, Nicki saw the back of the Land-Rover disappearing down the lane. Off to the pub, perhaps, she thought with relief, and then dismissed him from her mind.

Approaching the mill, she dropped Rowan in the carpark, intent on leaving without Robert knowing she was here. She couldn't face seeing him after last night, but Rowan's quick shout through the open door, that Nicki

71

had brought her home, brought Robert at once to the doorstep.

Nicki, still in the car, uncertain what to do or say, met his eyes and saw, in the long hard look he gave her, a question she knew she must answer.

'Time for a quick drink, Nicki?'

It was almost an order, and obediently she joined him and Rowan in the doorway. He put a hand on his daughter's shoulders propelling her down the passage.

'Go on in, love,' he said quietly. 'Let's try the elderflower champagne we made last year, shall we? Get the glasses out, and find the corkscrew.'

Then he turned to face Nicki. She trembled, seeing in his stern expression all the things she feared—bad thoughts of her and Leo, rejection of their own newly-blossoming friendship, but, surprisingly, he took her hand in his and gave her a brief smile.

'Don't look like that.'

There was a hint of amusement in his low voice.

'Like what?'

His hands were warm and strong and gradually she felt reassurance glow through her.

'Like a whipped dog. Although,' he added quizzically, 'I don't think anyone would have the courage to try and whip you, Nicki Bennett!'

Looking into his eyes, pale blue deepening into indigo, she read compassion, and knew he understood her problem.

'Nicki.'

His voice was vibrant, but very low, as if he spoke for her ears only.

'Yes, Robert?'

'I understand about last night. I know the sort of guy Leo Forman is.'

She watched his eyes grow dark and chilly, and shivered a little. He made a good enemy, no doubt of it. But he could also be a wonderful friend. Her mind wandered restlessly. As she looked at him, so his smile grew more intimate, and she knew that, despite all her hopeless fears, she and Robert were back in that warm, slowly developing relationship of mutual attraction which had drawn them together the first day they met. It was almost too good to believe.

He was studying her face, his eyes a kindlier blue now than she thought possible. He looked excited, almost aroused. Would he kiss her? But his next words were not what she anticipated.

'Good! You look better now, fit enough to hear my news.'

Her hands released, Nicki felt his mood change. Briskly he guided her towards the kitchen, at the far end of the shadowy passage.

'Come and toast the proposed sale of Grealy Mill,' he said exultantly. 'Laura and I have worked out an excellent deal. All that remains is for her business sponsor to approve it, and I want you to join in our celebrations!'

As he pushed open the kitchen door, he called out jovially, 'Laura! Nicki's here. Let's have a drink to giving good old Grealy Mill a new lease of life, and to your part in its restored future!'

Nicki had never heard him so cheerful or emotional. She wondered whether it was just the plans for the mill or the presence of Laura that had engendered his exuberance. Numbly, she entered the kitchen, invitingly warm and friendly, with April sunshine pouring in through the window.

'Hi,' Laura said coolly.

Dressed in a camel-coloured silk shirt, matching trousers, and with a tan leather jacket draped around the chair behind her, she looked very much at ease, Nicki thought resentfully.

'Come to join the party, have you?'

It was hardly a welcoming greeting, but Nicki nodded, sat down in the chair Robert pulled out, and retreated into a dismal world of disappointment and slow-building anger. How could she believe in Robert's growing affection for her, when, clearly, he and Laura were already embarked on a relationship of their own?

CHAPTER FOUR

London, despite its crowds and noise, seemed unbearably empty, Nicki thought morosely, as she dealt with the phone messages and faxes that had piled up over the weekend. However, with a restorative coffee at her side, she soon had it all under control.

It was already late afternoon, and she knew tomorrow would be hectic. A light snack and an early bed would surely get her back into work mode, and discipline and unruly emotions still threshing inside her.

Allowing them one final fling, she sat sipping her coffee and thinking back to leaving Devon. Only a few hours up the motorway, yet she was in a different world. She hadn't stayed long at the mill, for Robert's exuberance at finding a likely buyer, and Laura's unconcealed smiles in his direction had been hard to accept. So she had quickly returned to Rose Cottage, picked at Gee's roast dinner and then bade the family goodbye, promising to be back again soon.

Dad had held her close for a long moment, his voice gruff in her ears.

'Don't leave it too long. I'm not here for ever, you know.'

'Come on, Dad, who's the one always talking about positive thinking?' she had

75

joked, and was relieved to see him smile before she left.

Gee had been short, and to the point.

'I'll do all I can for your dad. At least you can trust me about that, honey.'

As she switched on the engine of the car, Leo bent his head over her.

'Don't be too hard on me, Nicko. Most people fight. Don't take it too seriously.'

His words reawakened an echo of their old, shared affection, and, without thinking any more of the trick he'd played on her recently, she'd lifted her face for his kiss. Togetherness, ruined by incompatibility, she thought sadly, driving away and leaving him in the lane, watching her go.

But that was all done with now. Resolutely, she forced herself to concentrate on the present. A huge work-load awaited her. Dealing with it would put paid to all the old dreams and new hopes.

And then, the next evening, relaxing after the wild day's problems, the phone rang.

'Nicki? It's me, Rowan.'

'How lovely to hear you! How's things?'

'OK, I suppose.'

Nicki waited, heartbeat suddenly unsteady.

'What news of the mill?' she asked, adding, 'And your dad?'

'He's OK. Terribly busy. He has an exhibition next week, so we don't have much time together. And anyway, Laura's in and

76

out.'

Rowan's grumpy tone indicated disapproval, and Nicki grinned sympathetically.

'I get bored,' Rowan complained, certainly sounding it. 'So I thought I'd ring you.'

Nicki's smile died. Well, better to be a substitute for boredom than entirely forgotten, she supposed wryly. But Rowan's next words gave her a great glow of pleasure.

'Actually, Dad said he must call you, but I said not to bother, I would.'

Rowan's voice took on a note of excitement.

'We want you to come to his birthday party, on the twelfth, that's Saturday. He and Laura are seeing the business guy who's buying the mill, so this is an important day. Do say you'll come, Nicki.'

'Try and keep me away!'

Nicki made herself sound enthusiastic, but had difficulty in controlling her racing thoughts. It would be great to see Robert again, but in the company of the all-powerful Laura? She remembered the cool disregard aimed at her at their last meeting. Then she grinned resolutely. Never mind! Robert wanted her there.

'I should love to come,' she said honestly. 'I'll stay at Rose Cottage. Dad wasn't too well when I rang last night.'

For a second her voice wobbled. It was becoming horribly clear that Dad's condition was slowly, but steadily, deteriorating.

77

'Oh, I forgot!' Rowan quickly made amends. 'Dad said do you think they'd both come as well, to the party? Mr Bennett and what do you call her? His Canadian wife?'

'Gee.' Nicki was smiling again. 'Tell Robert, please, that I'm quite sure they'd be happy to share his party.'

'Great! I'll go and see them after school tomorrow. 'Bye, Nicki. See you on Saturday, then.'

'Yes, but—'

Rowan had gone and, abruptly, Nicki felt a loneliness hit her, something she'd not felt for a long time. Suddenly getting up and pacing the floor, she came to terms with what she now knew was missing from her life. It was commitment, and a returned love. It seemed so little to ask. Most people found it, somehow. Even the most unlikely types. Look at Gee and Dad! Talk about chalk and cheese! But they had a loving companionship that kept Gee at his side, even though he was ill and increasingly demanding. Nicki wondered bleakly if she would ever find a man who could make her feel as Gee clearly felt for Dad.

At the window, staring blindly at the hurrying crowds and jammed traffic, Nicki thought of Leo, for whom she still felt reluctant affection, despite hating his tricks and ploys. And then she thought of Robert, Leo's complete opposite in every way. She knew she had a sort of love for both of them, in opposing ways. Leo said he needed her, but could she trust him for the rest of her life? And as for Robert, well, she knew he was trustworthy and perceptive, and infinitely compassionate and loving.

The words slid into her mind with immense impact. She nodded, and admitted silently that, given the chance, she could willingly give Robert the commitment she longed to receive herself. But how did she know that Robert really had any affection for her? There was Laura . . .

Leo was available. Robert was not. Face tense, and hands clenched, Nicki realised how impossibly complex life was. And then, out of the blue, just for a second, she thought back to the workshop at the mill, shamefacedly telling Robert her feelings about the old wheel. And he had understood.

'The heart of things,' he'd said, in his gravely, gentle voice, as if, she thought distractedly, the wheel was life itself.

Her mind cleared and she smiled. That was a good thought! The wheel, like life, forever churning up water, people and events, sometimes throwing them into quiet, forgotten backwaters, even finishing them off altogether at times. She shivered. But sometimes, and her smile widened, it threw people together, bringing sweet peace and love. The wheel was infinitely powerful, bringing both disasters and happiness and sweeping the world along in its unthinking wake. Now she understood how important it was to Robert and Rowan, and herself, to restore the old wheel at Grealy Mill.

A new, happier resolve flooded through her. She'd stay at Rose Cottage on Friday night, spending time with Dad, refusing to let Gee needle her, and then on Saturday she would help celebrate Robert's birthday. Seeing him again would help clear her mind, free her of doubt, one way or the other. Leo or Robert?

Then briskly she made a few decisions. Plan for the future! Buy a new dress. Book a smart haircut. Her mind centred, and quietened. What present could she buy Robert? Something unusual, to remind him of her, in case she never saw him again.

In the kitchen, preparing a salad for her evening meal, she frowned when the mobile blipped.

'Yes?' she said sharply, wishing she'd switched the wretched thing off.

'Nicko! Haven't eaten yet, have you?'

'Leo! What on earth are you doing up here?'

'Answer my question and calm down. You sound like a dog on the end of a chewed rope. Now, try again, darling.'

His charm was wry, the sound of his familiar voice a panacea to all the dark thoughts she had been conjuring up. At this moment she knew she could forgive him almost anything.

Sitting down in the kitchen rocking chair, cradling the phone, she grinned.

'OK. Here we go. No, I haven't eaten. But I'm just washing the lettuce.'

'Excellent. I'll bring all the bits and pieces, and the wine. Go and put on something pretty and make up your mind to be nice to me. Everything's wrong with my world at the moment.'

'What on earth's happened?'

'I'll tell you later, when I'm crying on your shoulder.'

But he didn't sound anywhere near to tears, she thought, the old suspicion creeping up on her.

'Now, go and wash that lettuce,' he ordered cheerfully. 'I'll be twenty minutes, no more.'

When he arrived, complete with bag of groceries, a bottle of wine and some spicy pizzas, Nicki was ready for him, her emerald silk shirt celebrating the occasion, smile quick and friendly. But for all her feeling of pleasure at his company on this lonely evening, she kept herself alert. It was always imperative, with Leo, to be prepared for any of his little games. Yet this particular game surprised her with its simplicity and lack of self-importance.

'The mill project's off,' Leo said casually, smiling approval of the homemade mayonnaise and refilling their wine glasses. 'Your friend Armstrong's got himself deeply in with the lovely Laura and her business master,

81

and so yours truly might as well think of something else to modernise.'

Nicki studied his bland expression. He sounded nonchalant, but she knew his ambition was vast. This put-down would have really injured his ego. How could he let it go so easily?

Carefully, helping herself to more salad, she said, 'Yes, I hear it's all as good as settled, or will be, come Saturday.'

Leo gave her a sharp look.

'Got your spies out, have you, darling?'

Despite herself, Nicki felt colour rise in her cheeks. He had always been able to irritate her.

'No spies, just Rowan, who likes to ring and chat.'

'Ah! The small Celt. Going to be a beauty one day. Nasty temper, though. Like her old man, I'd guess, wouldn't you, Nicko?'

She felt his eyes on her, knew that he was enjoying baiting her, but she refused to rise.

'I don't know Robert all that well, Leo,' she said, more calmly than she felt. 'I only met him a couple of times.'

Leo drained his glass.

'Just as well. I wouldn't want you to be disappointed. I mean, he's as good as living with the lovely Laura.'

He stared across the table, his smile one of sardonic amusement. Nicki got to her feet, scooping away the empty plates and turning towards the kitchen.

'Ice cream, or bananas?' she offered tersely.

Innocently, Leo said, 'I'll have them both,' and she swung round, unable to control herself any longer.

'Of course you will,' she snapped. 'Trust you to take everything that's going. Oh, Leo, what a brute you are! Why on earth are you here this evening? Not just to see what fun you can have at my expense, I'll be bound. There's sure to be some more devious reason for it!'

In the small, tense silence growing between them, she saw the expression in his eyes change. He was smiling, as he had done when they were young and in love, and just for a second her heart leaped. But then she remembered how she'd been through all this before. She was far too sensible now to let him entrap her all over again, wasn't she? Banging the sweet on the table, she sat down clumsily, avoiding his eyes.

'OK. Help yourself,' she muttered.

But Leo did no more than finger the bananas and shake his head.

'Only kidding,' he told her, apologetically enough to make her wonder if he didn't really mean it, for once. 'Look, Nicko, I came because I want you, and I needed to see you.'

'You don't want me, Leo. You never did.'

Her whisper was ignored.

'The truth is that I've decided to move on. The mill project hasn't come up to scratch, so

83

I'm back in town making other contacts, other plans, and Canada calls me home. I'll be here for a week or so, and then off. The thing is, Nicko—'

He stopped, reached over the table and captured her hand in his. His eyes were unreadable, but she saw tension in his face.

'I need you to come with me, Nicko.'

The unexpected words hung in the air like a shaft of light illuminating her confused mind. She met his unblinking, expectant stare and felt herself unbalanced. It was too much, too soon, and just when she was at her most vulnerable. Briefly, foolishly, she wondered if he could have read her thoughts just before he phoned, when she had felt so unsure about her choice of possible partners.

'Well? Not like you to run out of words.'

He smiled, fingers stroking the back of her cold hand. She could almost believe that he did truly need her. But the word love hadn't been mentioned. And then something clicked in the recesses of her thoughts. Two can play at this game. Defensively, she slid her hand out of his, smiled back at him, and lowered her eyes flirtatiously.

'Why, thank you kindly, sir, she said.'

Her voice was amused and steady, satisfactorily concealing all the disturbance within her.

'Only, you see, I happen to have a home and a career of my own, right here in London. And my poor old dad in Devon—'

Her overbright voice faded as she saw the compression of his lips, and remembered that it was Leo who made the jokes, never his victim.

'Leo,' she said urgently, forced into unplanned words by the emotions swamping her, 'that was rotten of me. I'm sorry. You asked me to go away with you, and I thank you for asking. But, I can't. It's just not possible.'

For a long moment he held her gaze, then, almost carelessly, he picked up his wine glass, twisting it between his long fingers and staring at her over the crystal rim.

'I see,' he said quietly. 'Mm, yes, I think I do see. You've fallen for that Celtic savage down in Devon, haven't you?'

She watched his eyes narrow, saw the hint of emotion that had been visible before. He put the glass on the table and picked up a banana. Helplessly, she watched him peeling it, and felt it was her own skin he was stripping.

'Excellent!' he commented, with a grin, as he began to eat it. 'All that potassium! Nothing for you, my darling?'

She feared the mocking note in the foolish words, and shook her head. Leo's grin broadened.

'Silly girl! You'll need building up if you plan to do battle with the alarming Laura, you know!'

Suddenly courage returned, along with the

kindling of quick anger. How dare he treat her like this! Getting to her feet, she glowered at him.

'Look, Leo, if you came to play nasty games, then you can go again. I don't need any of this. And how I choose to live my life has nothing to do with you at all!'

Slowly he rose, pushing the chair beneath the table before he turned to look quizzically at her.

'I see that now. Guess I just made a mistake, didn't I?'

His hand reached for hers, and although her quick reaction was to step back, she still recalled the old Leo and allowed him to take it in his.

'One more mistake, Nicko. The pattern of my life. First the mill, and now you. Must be slipping.'

For a second his eyes lit up with mischief, and he pressed her hand before releasing it.

'But I've still got a few tricks up my sleeve. Never say die, eh, darling?'

'Goodbye, Leo. I'm sorry it couldn't have worked for us.'

She shrugged helplessly, and he nodded, raising a mocking eyebrow and hooking up his jacket before swinging out of the flat, out of her life? Nicki wondered whether she was glad or miserable. Leo had always had that effect on her. Hard to forget that they'd loved, once, and now, increasingly, as she understood his complex personality better, she felt sorry for him.

Tilting her chin, she cleared the supper dishes. It was high time she erased Leo Forman from her life and got on with living.

For the next few days, work engulfed her. There was an important contract to be prepared for the new venues they were advertising in West Sussex, and an appointment to view possible accommodation on the Downs near Brighton. Good to be busy, she told herself, to be too weary at night to even think about Robert, or Leo. But, by the middle of the week, she knew she must prepare for Robert's birthday party.

She was driving home, late that afternoon, passenger seat piled high with purchases she'd spent two whole hours choosing, when a discreet sign in a gallery window close at hand caught her eye. Braking behind a conveniently stopping bus, she read it with mounting pleasure.

EXHIBITION OF WOOD SCULPTURE BY ROBERT ARMSTRONG.

She just had time to see the dates advertised, a week hence, when the bus pulled out, and she was rudely reminded to move on by the traffic behind her. Instantly, her mind was re-energised. This was the exhibition Robert had mentioned when they first met.

87

She wondered foolishly if he would invite her to the opening, but knew that it was unlikely. But she would go and see his work. Then she remembered Laura, and her pleasure diminished.

She drove home faster than usual, telling herself that Leo had only been baiting her by hinting Laura had moved in with Robert. Perhaps it was, after all, only a business relationship. And yet, suddenly her blue skies were cloudy and grey. Ridiculous! She and Robert were merely acquaintances, with a shared urge to restore the old mill. But she knew, deep inside, that it was more than that.

In the flat, she flung her carrier bags on to the bed and then stood still in the middle of the room. Maybe she shouldn't go to the party, after all. What if Robert thought her a moon-eyed, gauche creature, who was chasing him?

Desperately, she unwrapped the new clothes. In the boutique, the gleaming silk trousers, with matching skimpy camisole top, had seemed exactly right, but here, in her own home, and with increasing envy of Laura, wasn't it just a bit bright, the brilliant blues and sea-greens rather overpowering? Even a bit too trendy and eye-catching? How could it possibly compete with Laura's subtle elegance?

Picking up the whispering silk suit, Nicki draped it around her body, and stared into the long mirror. But all she saw was the image of

Robert's face, half-turned from her, as he worked at the wood beneath his big, careful hands, and she knew that, come what may, she couldn't stop herself going to the party at the mill on Saturday.

Putting the suit away carefully, she got herself a glass of white wine and a sandwich and sat by the window in the front room, trying to sort out her confused thoughts. Before she went to bed, much later, she had come to a bleak acceptance of facts. Everything would depend on Robert's welcome of her at the weekend, or his lack of it. She would know, within seconds, once she saw them together, if he and Laura were really in love.

Leaving home next morning, she took the few envelopes the postman handed her and riffled through them, going down in the lift to the garage. There was a bill, a letter from an old client, who had wanted to keep in touch, and a thick, cream-coloured envelope, holding a thick, cream-coloured card.

Robert Armstrong requests the pleasure of your presence at the Gallery Myfany in New Street where he is holding an exhibition of his latest work.

Nicki leaned against her car and found she was breathing too fast for comfort. But she was smiling, and happiness filled her. For beneath the elegant print were a few words written in a large, sprawling hand, by Robert himself.

Nicki—do hope you'll come. Important that

you do, but we'll be meeting before then. Rowan says you're coming to the mill on Saturday. Should have rung you myself, but busy, busy. Robert.

The sun shone brightly, and the morning traffic did nothing to halt Nicki's great surge of joy. Robert hadn't said a word about Laura. Could Leo have been wrong? Well, she thought, as she parked outside the office and grabbed her briefcase, everything would become plain on Saturday.

And, oh, she was so glad she'd bought that trendy, beautiful silk suit!

CHAPTER FIVE

'He insists on going,' Gee said anxiously. 'I've tried to persuade him not to but, well, you know your dad. Once his mind is made up.' She smiled bleakly. 'He said, 'I'll go to that party if it kills me!' He's a determined man, is Harry Bennett.'

Nicki nodded sympathetically.

'I know he is. So where is he now?'

'Resting. I actually got him into bed for the afternoon. He was tired after that walk you had this morning. But he made me promise to call him in good time. Oh, this damned party! Why do we have to go?'

Gee turned away, but not before Nicki had

seen the concern on her face.

'Because Dad wants to. And it'd be stressful if you didn't let him.'

Nicki didn't add that it was also because she wanted to go. Dad had agreed that Robert's birthday must be celebrated, adding, with a mysterious half-smile, 'I've got a present for him. Must deliver it in person.'

Looking at Gee, she suggested, 'Let's have a wander round the garden,' and hesitantly put her hand on Gee's taut shoulder. 'You know what Aunt Rachel says. She insists that herbs help you relax. Come on, Gee, let's give it a try!'

In the cool, dimly-lit passageway, Gee met her gaze. She sniffed, switched on the familiar, faintly malevolent grin, and said acidly, 'Trust Rachel to be full of old wives' tales! But OK, anything to help my headache.'

Leading the way, she walked through the conservatory and into the long, shrub-sheltered garden, its daffodils and tulips bright in the afternoon sun, and a breeze-touched fragrance drifting up from the herb bed.

Stress, Nicki thought, following Gee to the wooden seat in the centre of the circular bed. I've never known her to be worried like this before. And then, as she sat down beside her stepmother, a surprising thought followed. I've never really known her, have I? But I'm beginning to—at last.

Carefully, she tried to get Gee to talk. It

91

wasn't easy at first, but words stumbled, and then flowed.

'Of course, all that hassle about buying the mill upset Harry. When you were last down, and he realised what Leo and I planned to do, I didn't think he'd be so upset. It wasn't quite what he had in mind, you see. If only I'd thought about it. I blame myself so much,' she said huskily.

Nicki caught the scent of the mint surrounding them both with its fresh sharpness and took a deep breath. This was an opportunity to get closer to Gee.

Carefully, she said, 'But, Gee, you know that Dr Marten said you must expect Dad's condition to deteriorate, anyway. Really, you shouldn't take the blame.'

Gee slanted a quick look sideways.

'Yeah, I know. But I do blame myself, and Leo. You see, Nicki, I realise that—that I'm going to be alone when Harry goes.'

Nicki kept silent as the words registered. But Gee was going on.

'And another thing. It's Leo! Not exactly supportive, is he? Not what I'd hoped at all. Once he knew this mill project wasn't coming off, he just disappeared. Had to go back to town, he said, new contracts, couldn't afford to hang about down here. Not a word about did I need him. And he's been stirring up trouble down here. Not sure how, but there's talk in the village. He's been seen chatting to that old man who lives by the mill.'

'Archie Luscombe?'

Gee nodded.

'That's the guy. Crazy, if you ask me. What Leo could want with him I can't imagine, can you?'

'No.'

Nicki set her lips firmly. She didn't even want to guess what Leo was up to with old Archie.

'How's your head?' she asked, intent on changing the subject, and was amazed to see Gee's broad smile.

'You know what? Must be something in Rachel's old tales after all! I do believe it's better.'

'Great. Then we've just got time for a cuppa before we wake Dad and get into our glad rags ready for the party!'

Nodding, Gee got to her feet. She gave Nicki a long look, before saying slowly, 'I haven't talked like this before. You know what, honey, it's not just Rachel's old herbs, I think it's you being nice to me as well!'

Nicki met the wry gaze with honesty.

'About time, isn't it, Gee? I haven't exactly been the most helpful stepdaughter, have I?'

Gee set her bright smile in place as she walked down the garden and into the cottage.

'Guess we'll call a truce, shall we? Hey, I'm making lots of new friends! Young Rowan, and now you.'

93

They smiled at each other with fresh understanding, before Gee said mischievously, 'And now, tell me what you're wearing to the party, Cinderella?'

Nicki caught up the warmer mood, and laughed.

'Wait and see! I'm definitely going to be the belle of this particular ball!'

She went upstairs with a spark of new determination. She was going to look her best this evening, come what may.

'Dad, are you awake? Can I come in?' she called as she passed his room later on her way downstairs.

Time to see that he was fit enough to enjoy the outing, and to make the most of the little time they had together. He was sitting in a chair by the window, already dressed in his dark grey suit and striped shirt. His smile, as she entered, was warm, filling her with relief. Just for a second she forgot his pallor, and the fact that he was no longer the big-framed giant he had once been.

'Dad, how smart you look! I'm thrilled that you and Gee are coming this evening.'

She took his hand and smiled into his serene eyes.

'Try and stop us! You look great, too, Nicki. I like that young man at the mill. He called in last week, to collect Rowan who was weeding the herbs in the garden, and we had a most interesting chat about his work, and about his

94

plans for restoring the old place. Sounds good, if all goes well, that is.'

'From what I hear, everything will be signed and sealed very soon,' Nicki said quietly.

She'd known all along that Dad and Robert would get on. She added enthusiastically, 'He's having an exhibition in town next week, and he's actually invited me to go.'

Harry Bennett looked at his daughter. Something new about the independent, loving Nicki he thought perceptively. There was a new, warmer depth. Could it be that, at last, she'd met the right man? He smiled to himself and pressed her hand, as he prepared to say words that were difficult, but necessary.

'I'd like to think that you were settled, Nicki, love, before I—move on.'

He saw the colour rise in her cheeks, before it faded, leaving her pale and anxious. His voice rose as he went on.

'This Robert Armstrong, now . . .'

And then abruptly he stopped, shaking his head at her suddenly wary eyes. He grinned fondly.

'No business of mine? I don't intend to play the heavy father! You're a big girl, not my baby any longer. Now, if you'll just find my best party shoes, bottom of the wardrobe, I think, I can get out of the way before Gee comes in from the bathroom, wanting all the space!'

Nicki found the shoes, helped him on with them, and then escorted him downstairs. She

95

said nothing, but her mind was busy. Dad had said two very important things—he hinted that he'd guessed her feelings for Robert, and, more solemnly, that he knew he wasn't going to live very much longer.

As she took his arm, walking slowly down the garden while they waited for Gee, she felt very close to him and knew that words were unnecessary. Instinctively she sensed that this weekend, this particular evening, was a special time, and was determined that they should both make the best of it.

The mill was bright with Chinese lanterns and small candlelit lamps fixed on to its shabby outside walls. As Gee parked the Land-Rover among the other cars, Nicki heard soft music drifting out from the open door and windows, and felt her spirits rise in expectation. Soon she would be with Robert.

The excitement of the moment made her almost forget to pick up the present she had bought for him, an old, calf-bound book describing William Morris's philosophy of life and work. Seeing it in an antique shop last week, she had thought it was the very thing for Robert. Now she carried it in her hand, approaching the millhouse.

Rowan ran out to greet them as they neared the door. She looked pretty in a pale green dress that made a flame out of her abundant hair.

'Hi! Come on in. Oh, Nicki, don't you look

great? Love that colour!'

Well, Nicki thought wryly, at least someone approves! Gee had raised an eyebrow when she saw the bright trouser suit, quickly offering the loan of a shawl, in case it got cold later on! Nicki had thought the offer two-handed, but hadn't risen to the bait.

Laura stood by the open doorway, her beaded, midnight blue slip of a dress breathtaking in its simplicity.

'Good to see you all,' she drawled coolly, not meeting Nicki's eyes. 'Do go on in and make yourselves at home.'

Nicki was about to ask where Robert was, when Laura's head turned to greet a new arrival.

'Carl!' she called over Nicki's shoulder. 'Great to see you. I knew you'd come if you possibly could.'

The tone was warm, the smile rapturous, and Nicki wondered how anyone could change so quickly, as she watched Laura lead the stocky, balding man into the house, talking animatedly as they went.

'Such good manners,' Gee commented sarcastically. 'Guess we'll just have to make our own way. Nicki, find a seat for your dad. I'm not having him standing all evening.'

Leaving Gee and Dad comfortably settled in the warm kitchen, talking to some old friends, Nicki wandered off. She'd put her present for Robert in a space on the bookcase beneath the window. Suddenly she felt shy about giving it to him personally. Better let him find it after they'd all left.

Exploring the old building, she found that one of the near-derelict rooms had been opened and redecorated for the party. Chairs, small tables and a couple of sofas had been arranged in the wide, ground-floor area that had once been filled with wooden machinery and storage space.

Her mind easily conjured up images of the past. Sacks of corn had been winched up these old walls, pulled through the opening on the top floor and then fed into hoppers, to be ground into flour by the great stone wheels which were attached to the long, vertical shaft running through the building, powered by the water wheel outside. Now the great room was half-empty, save for rough beams, and a flight of worn, wooden stairs, leading upwards to the next floor.

She stood still, staring at the limewashed walls, sadly neglected over the years. But it was simple to imagine that the ancient building was still in use. For a second she thought she felt the vibration of the machinery, heard the creak of the wheel, and the ceaseless wash of water, falling from paddle to paddle, then flowing on, into the millrace beyond the buildings.

Then, suddenly, Robert was at her side, his hand on her bare arm, his welcoming smile making her catch her breath.

'Hello, Nicki Bennett! I've missed you.'

Somehow, she regained her poise.

'That's nice! And I've missed this wonderful old mill.'

And you, she wanted to add, stopping just in time.

'You look wonderful,' he said, his eyes moving over her, and he added, very low, 'The halcyon lady herself.'

'Halcyon?'

'A Celtic legend, Nicki, about the kingfisher, called the halcyon bird, with plumage of that same fantastic blue-green that you're wearing. It suits you so extraordinarily well.'

She had no words, just a sense of everything being right now they were together. She thought Robert had never looked so attractive. The shabby polo sweater and jeans she was used to were replaced now with a dark green corduroy jacket, matching trousers and a linen shirt, and his eyes reflected some of the same sober colouring.

They gazed at her with a warmth that made her colour rise, and she was content just to stand beside him, sharing what she fervently hoped was a mutual pleasure at being together again—until voices broke into their silence.

'Robert, come and meet Carl Christie.'

Laura's tone was imperative. She took no notice of Nicki.

'He's made such an enormous effort to be

here tonight. Not many sponsors drive two hundred miles to meet their future craftsmen!'

The tone was jokey, even patronising, and Nicki wondered angrily how Robert would react. He raised an apologetic eyebrow at her, and murmured, very low, 'Sorry, but you see how things are,' before turning, to hold out his hand to the waiting businessman.

'Good to meet you at last, Armstrong,' the stocky man said, small eyes narrowing shrewdly. 'Time we had a talk, eh?'

Nicki watched Laura escort them out of sight, and guessed they had retreated to Robert's studio. She went in search of Rowan, eventually finding her and Gemma busy in the kitchen.

'Nicki! Can you help?'

Rowan's face was flushed as she bent down to take a tray of sausage rolls from the Aga.

'Of course. What can I do?'

'Take these quiches into the big room, and then come back for the plates.'

'Have you done all this yourself?' Nicki asked, minutes later.

Rowan wiped her hands and smiled proudly.

'Gemma and me. Your dad lent me a book about herbs, and Gee, sorry, Mrs Bennett, gave me some recipes.'

Nicki wondered at such an unexpected friendship, and then decided it was probably good for both of them.

'I can't wait to start eating,' she said

100

cheerily. 'It all smells and looks absolutely fabulous. You must give me a few tips sometime.'

The evening melted into warmth, friendliness and increasing noise as voices hummed and laughed, and music drifted in and out of the conversations. Nicki saw brief glimpses of Laura and Robert mingling with their guests. She saw the man called Carl looking at his watch and downing glasses of orange juice, and wondered if he was preparing for the return drive to London. No doubt his visit here had been to put the final seal on the contract Laura had prepared for the sale of the mill. He and Robert must have been discussing the plans for its restoration, and Laura had been with them, all the time. She still was.

Nicki's thoughts grew despondent. Clearly Robert needed Laura to organise his business deals. Perhaps a dominating and efficient partner meant more to him than a truly loving companion.

No good thinking like this, she told herself briskly. Reality must be faced, and although she had enjoyed the evening, it had shown her quite clearly where Robert's allegiance lay. Shrugging off her unhappiness, she went into the kitchen, to find Gee in the doorway.

'There you are! Guess it's time we moved. Harry's tired. He's been talking to Robert. He looks so pale. I think he's overdone the chatting.'

Gee's voice was low, the words urgent, and Nicki said at once, 'Give me the keys. I'll bring the Land-Rover to the door. Can you get Dad there by yourself?'

'Leave it to me.'

Gee handed over the keys and went back to where Harry sprawled untidily in his chair.

'Ups-a-daisy, honey! Time to go home.'

As Nicki halted the Land-Rover outside the millhouse door, there was a sudden blast of noise. She got out, stared around, and was shocked at what she saw. Small, flickering flames had burst out of the pretty lanterns and lamps hanging on the walls. There was a menacing, crackling noise, a smell of fire, and a terrible sense of danger.

'Fire!' she screamed, dashing into the house, almost knocking people down in her rush to alert them. 'Fire! Get outside! Robert! Laura!'

Panic struck, and Nicki prayed that Gee and Dad were safe. But she couldn't go back to find out. She must get to a phone, must raise the alarm, and save the mill from destruction. Laura's mobile lay on the table just inside the door, and Nicki punched 999 with frantic fingers as Robert came to her side.

'Good girl.'

He was shepherding his guests out of various doors.

'Take it quietly,' he told them, voice clear

and authoritative. 'The fire brigade will be here at any moment, and once outside, you're safe. Just stay away from the walls.'

As he headed for the well at the far end of the courtyard, bucket in hand, he shouted to Nicki, 'Thank goodness you saw what was going on.'

His smile was brief, but helped ease the terrible shock that still filled her. Seeing that everybody was now out of the building, she went to find Gee, who had backed the Land-Rover, with Dad in it, to a safe distance. Gee leaned out of the window.

'Come on,' she ordered. 'Let's get home. Harry should be in bed. I've given him one of his tablets, but he doesn't look too good.'

Nicki saw and heard the anxiety she felt, but said firmly, 'I must stay here, Gee. See if I can help.'

'Help?' Gee was shouting now. 'It's your dad who needs your help, my girl. The mill must take its chance. I can't run the risk with Harry.'

Meekly, Nicki climbed into the Land-Rover. Gee was right, of course. Her place was with her family, but her heart, and her thoughts, longed desperately to stay at the mill, to be near Robert, in this moment of disaster.

The next day passed in a flurry of doctor's visits, of taking Harry to the local hospital some four miles away, sitting with him, supporting Gee while tests were made, and,

103

finally, trying to discover how badly the mill had been damaged.

Nicki, restlessly preparing a meal for herself and Gee in the early evening, longed to be there. Wildly, she wondered why no news had filtered through the village grapevine, but of course it was Sunday and no-one was about. But why hadn't Robert phoned, or Rowan? Were they both safe?

Taking one of Gee's pasties out of the freezer and peeling potatoes for chips, Nicki's imagination ran riot. Supposing Robert had gone back into his studio to retrieve some of his work. What if the fire had got such a hold that a wall collapsed on him?

It's no good, she told herself wretchedly. I'll go mad if I don't find out soon. I'll phone.

But there was no reply and she was left guessing that the line was down. Supper was silent, with Gee picking at her food and refilling her wine glass too often. Neither could Nicki eat. At length their eyes met across the table.

'Waiting's agony. I'd rather know the worst than have to endure more of this,' Gee said.

Nicki smiled stiffly.

'Just keep hoping,' she suggested. 'Dr Marten said Dad was putting up a good fight.'

'Yeah, he's always been a fighter. He sure is an example to us both.'

Pushing aside her plate, she rose.

'So I'm fighting! I'm going upstairs to sort

104

out his clothes, ready to bring him home just as soon as they give us the OK!'

At the door she turned.

'And why aren't you fighting, too, honey? I guess your fight's a different one from mine, but you could still try and win it. On your feet! That Laura woman's OK when it comes to organisation, but I reckon poor old Robert needs a shoulder to lean on, right now.'

Minutes later, wondering at Gee's unexpected perception, Nicki grabbed her car keys, then paused at the front door as the phone in the hall rang. Her heart jumped. Could it be Robert? But it was Leo.

'Hi, darling. How's things?'

She set her lips, grinding out an irritated reply.

'What d'you want?'

'Come on!' His voice was smoothly seductive. 'Only asking a civil question. Want the village gossip, that sort of thing. Births, deaths, marriages?' He paused, then added gently, 'Disasters, perhaps?' and instantly she knew what he meant.

'Leo! The mill! It was something to do with you!'

'Not me, love. Hundreds of miles away, wasn't I?'

The amusement in his tone made her fury rise.

'Of course you've got an alibi! You always had!'

Her mind raced. What had Gee said? That Leo had been hobnobbing with crazy Archie Luscombe? And Leo himself had hinted about having a trick up his sleeve.

'You set him up,' she shouted furiously. 'That old man, he had a fixation about the mill, so you got him to actually set fire to it!'

'My darling girl,' he drawled, 'you can't hold me responsible for a madman's actions. Even you can't do that! I mean the guy's a real firebrand, isn't he?' He chuckled. 'In more ways than one, I'd say!'

'Leo, you're a vile, scheming, hateful creature and I never want to speak to you again.'

'Come on, Nicko, don't go on at me. Remember what I said the other night? Well, I'm just fighting to get what I want so badly, and that's you, my darling.'

'Get lost!'

Slamming down the receiver, she stood in the hall, thoughts whirling. Intuition had warned her about that evening, just as it had about Leo and his cunning plans. Did Robert know who was responsible for firing the mill? If not, she knew she must tell him, difficult though it would be. And did Robert still half-believe she and Leo were an item? What a muddle this all was.

She let herself out into the quiet, scented night. She must find Robert and face up to this impossible situation. As she swept into the mill carpark, uncertain about arriving at this time of night, she saw in the headlights a tall, still figure, standing a short distance away. Robert stood alone, looking at the ruin of his home and his dreams.

The night was lit by a half-moon, its beams shafting down through the trees, casting shadows and creating a mysterious atmosphere. Jumping out of the car she walked towards the motionless figure.

'Robert?' she said hesitantly.

He turned slowly as she approached, but said nothing. At his side she was uncertain what to do or say. It was a heart-searing moment. Then he moved, and his arms went around her, holding her tightly.

'You've come,' he muttered, his voice almost inaudible, the warmth of his breath thawing her chilling anxiety. 'I've never felt so alone in my whole life, not even after Jane went off, leaving me and Rowan on our own.'

His arms enclosed her and she could hear the beat of his heart in time with her own. Raising his head, he held her a little apart, staring into her eyes, allowing her to see his face. She thought he was very pale, but perhaps it was only the moonlight. Certainly his eyes reflected the silvery beams, but it was his expression that made her already heightened emotions surge.

Gone was the enthusiasm that she admired when first they met. Now his face was set in hard lines, his mouth tightly compressed. All the optimism had vanished, and she was disturbed at the dullness of his gaze as he looked at her.

Quickly she said, 'Thank goodness you're safe! Is Rowan all right? Where is she?'

'Staying with the Joneses. She's shocked, but, yes, she's all right.'

His tone was flat and Nicki sought for words.

'I've been so worried. I couldn't come earlier, and the phone's out of order.'

Robert stepped away, threw an arm around her shoulders, and drew her towards the millhouse.

'I knew you'd be here when you could,' he said quietly. 'I heard that your father is in hospital.'

Robert's arm tightened around her as he saw the anxiety on her face.

'He's a gallant man. He won't give up without a fight,' he said.

'I'll tell Dad what you said when I see him tomorrow.'

By now they stood in the millhouse doorway, and she could see, by the light of his torch, the state of the damaged building. The door was burned, a segment of wall had collapsed, and dirty, charring marks stained everything in sight.

'It's terrible. Oh, Robert, I'm so sorry.'

'Yes, it's a wreck, isn't it? But it doesn't
108

really matter now.'

'Not matter?'

She looked at him sharply.

'The deal's fallen through. I've lost my buyer.'

Suddenly he seemed to come to life again, walking away from her, so that she had to follow him out into the moonlit courtyard.

'Robert, what on earth do you mean?'

She pulled at his arm, forcing him to turn and look at her. His eyes were deep pools, unreadable in their darkness.

'Christie decided that the mill was too badly damaged to be viable. In other words, his investment wouldn't pay off. And, of course, the fire didn't exactly help.'

Nicki was silent for a long moment. Her mind raced, and she knew this was the moment of truth. She took a deep breath.

'Robert,' she said slowly, 'I'm so desperately sorry. You must feel wretched, but there's something I have to tell you.'

She felt his gaze and wondered how to go on. Damn Leo and his tricks! But she spoke slowly, picking her words instinctively and praying they were the right ones.

'The fire wasn't an accident, Robert. It was Archie Luscombe again. I—'

He interrupted her.

'I guessed that. He'd poured paraffin over a couple of the lamps. The firemen found the can close by.'

Nicki shut her eyes and said bravely, 'But he was only doing what Leo told him to do.'

Out of the suddenly tense silence, Robert asked slowly,' How do you know?' and she shivered at his bitter tone.

His face was impassive, as the shadows shifted in the moonlight and she tried to read his emotions in vain.

'He rang me, just before I came here.'

Robert took a step backwards.

'Leo Forman? Your friend?'

She heard the ice in the words and forced herself to keep calm.

'Not my friend any longer.'

Somehow she must make him understand.

'He was furious when you wouldn't sell the mill to him and Gee. You see, this was his way of getting back at you, and at me.'

She felt his brooding stare, and shut her eyes to avoid it.

'Why at you, Nicki?' he asked, with a note of cold curiosity. 'Why should he want to do that? After all, I thought you and he were fond of each other.'

'We were, once. And Leo still is fond of me.'

There was no reply, and she rushed on foolishly, praying he would understand, and fearful that he would not.

'So he says, but I'm not . . . '

Silence, only her heart racing in the silence. She heard Robert sigh. He moved away, and she understood that he was distancing himself from her. All the joy of being with him, of having his arms around her, of hearing his pleasure at seeing her vanished and she felt weary and dispirited. Of course he had no feeling for her. Why should he?

But Robert hadn't finished. He returned to her side, and looked at her without saying anything. And then, abruptly, he reached out his hand, long, hard fingers running gently down her cheek, as he muttered unsteadily, 'I can forgive Leo Forman, and Archie, but you—part and parcel of it? No, that's hard to accept.'

She forced herself to be unemotional.

'You know, surely you must know, how much I want to see the mill restored, and the wheel in use again. Of course I had nothing to do with Leo's plans.'

'The wheel—ah, yes, the symbol of life.'

It seemed as if he was talking to himself and she had to listen intently. His hand dropped to his side. She watched him straighten his tall back, and raise his head to look at the moon overhead. There was a moment of almost relaxed concentration, and then he spoke in his familiar, vibrant voice, and with a casualness that astounded her.

'Just have to make the best of things, I suppose. I shall get the insurance for the fire damage, and of course I shan't bring charges against Archie, He's confused and old, and it seems everything got too much for him. I hear

111

he's going back to Kent, to be near his daughter. So I shall have the cottage to sell as well as this old clapped-out ruin.'

Nicki heard herself excluded from any feelings he may have once wanted to share, and which were now safely hidden again. Pain hit hard. Lifting her head, she spoke numbly.

'And Leo? What about him? You'll bring a court case against him?'

'The guy's not worth bothering with,' Robert answered coldly. 'Not in my opinion.' Turning, he gave her a hard look. 'But, of course, you may think differently.'

'No,' Nicki answered vehemently, 'I know what Leo is.'

She set her lips but said no more. What more could she say to convince Robert? It seemed quite clear that he had decided to condemn her.

Crushing back the pain that spread through her, she said quickly, before renewed emotion got the better of her, 'Well, at least the mill isn't completely ruined. You can still restore it, once you get the insurance money.'

'No, I'm moving out.'

Robert's tone was resolute and almost impersonal. Nicki felt she had suddenly become a stranger, and was being given the cold facts of something in which she was not involved. He looked down into her face. She saw his vivid eyes were deeply shadowed and she sensed a moment of final indecision within him.

Then he said steadily, 'Laura's persuaded me that it would be better to find a studio in London. Hopefully, the exhibition next week will bring in new contacts and some commissions, so Rowan and I will be making a fresh start, away from here.'

For a moment she was too shocked to speak, and then, 'Laura!' she exploded, staring up at him and feeling fury replace the pain.

'Laura!' she repeated harshly. 'I see! You've got it all worked out, haven't you? Leo and me, and you and Laura. Well, if that's how you want it, good luck to you!'

She ran towards the car. She couldn't stay here a moment longer. She had completely misunderstood Robert's attitude to her. It had been one of idle friendship, and that was all.

Slamming the door of her car she called back to him, 'I wish you well, Robert, you and Rowan. And Laura, of course.'

Robert's face, in the fitful moonlight, seemed to be concerned.

'Nicki? You'll come to the exhibition? I'll see you there?'

'Sorry,' she shouted back, 'but I'm staying down here, to be with Dad and Gee,' and before he could say any more she sped away.

CHAPTER SIX

During the next few days life was ever busier, and Nicki was thankful for it. Telephoning her London office on Monday morning, and requesting some of the holiday time due to her, she was given a couple of projects in Devon to deal with.

'Yes, of course I'll do them. Tavistock and Barnstaple? No problem.'

Once Dad was home from hospital, he could come with her on the assignments. The countryside was beautiful, and they would be together. Somehow, she forced Robert and that last, grim meeting, to the back of her mind, concentrating on helping Gee.

'Thank goodness you're here, honey. I'd be lost without you,' she kept saying.

Nicki's misery was slightly reduced by Gee's changed attitude, and she did all she could to foster the new, affectionate relationship growing between them. They visited Harry every day and were encouraged by his slow, but steady recovery.

'Another few days, the doctor said, and I'll be home. Can't wait!'

Harry's colour was better, his strength more evident, as he walked purposefully from the ward to the day room and back.

On the first day of Robert's exhibition,

Nicki was on business and drove both Gee and her father to Tavistock. The old grey buildings shone in the sun, the lanes were starred with primroses, and she told herself sternly that she was on the way to forgetting Robert. Almost, but not quite—she had to work hard to banish images of him and Laura at the exhibition.

Rowan, staying with her friend, Gemma, since the fire, had been dropping in most afternoons on her way back from school. She had an easy, happy relationship with Harry, and Nicki was delighted to see that an equally strong friendship with Gee had been built.

'Dad's still in London,' Rowan told Nicki on the last day of the exhibition. 'He phoned last night. He's got some commissions and he sounded excited. Brilliant, isn't it?'

Nicki longed to ask if Laura had found the studio he had mentioned, and also if Rowan knew about the intended move, but kept silent. It was no business of hers, not any more. Instead, she amused Rowan by demanding recipes of the vegetarian dishes that Rowan was so good at concocting.

'Simple ones, please,' she warned with a grin.

Later in the week, on the trip to Barnstaple, Nicki had Harry to herself, Gee being involved in a village bring-and-buy sale. By now, he was weary of being considered an invalid, and seemed so much better that Nicki's hope of a complete recovery seemed possible. As they drove back to Rose Cottage in the late afternoon, he asked her to call in at the mill.

'Just to look at it,' he said casually. 'Let's see how bad it is, shall we?'

Staring at the fire-scorched old building, Nicki felt a great lump in her throat. She hadn't wanted to come here. Every stone and stick reminded her of Robert's bitter rejection of her,

But when Harry said slowly, 'Doesn't seem too bad. Restoration is still possible,' she could no longer hold in her feelings.

'Robert's leaving,' she said huskily. 'Moving to London. He doesn't care what happens to the mill any longer.'

Harry was silent and she blinked away the threatening tears, until he said, 'Well, someone ought to care, don't you think so, love?'

Nicki nodded and Harry went on, 'I told your Robert—'

'He's not mine,' she snapped wretchedly.

'Hm. I see.' Harry's wise gaze took in her unhappiness, 'Anyway,' he continued, 'I told Robert that I was intending to make a donation towards the restoration. Always wanted to see that wheel turning again before I die,' he said slowly, and with a nostalgic smile. 'Told him that at the party. My present to him, really. He seemed glad at the time.'

Nicki didn't know what to say. Her father looked at her shrewdly.

'Given up, love, have you?' he asked gently.

'Not like you. Try a bit harder, why not? Never know what fate has in store, do you?'

Sighing, trying to meet his smile, she drove the car out into the lane again, and returned to Rose Cottage. She agreed with Dad, of course she did, but to try and get Robert back seemed a losing battle, remembering his words at their last meeting.

The next day was cloudy, with showers of rain. She filled the afternoon with paper work, and then, seeing the grey sky clearing, decided to get some fresh air. Her head ached, and everything seemed especially miserable.

Never mind, she thought, as she went down the cottage path, next week I'll be back in London. I'll make a new life, somehow. As she crossed the road, heading for the footpath, she thought she heard the phone ringing in Rose Cottage but ignored it. The office could wait until tomorrow. The path was muddy after the morning rain, but it was wonderful to be out here, the sun overhead, and the sea a far-distant blur of grey-blue. Nature certainly put human troubles into perspective, she thought wryly, and found she was able to smile with some of her old contentment.

Then suddenly, coming round the corner of the field, in the middle of the footpath, a man appeared—a tall figure, looking at his feet as he walked, striding out as if he were late for a date. Robert! What should she do? It was too late to run. She stopped, watched him lift his head and see her. Like her, he stood motionless for a moment. Then he raised an arm, waved and came forward with ever quickening steps.

'Nicki! Thank goodness!'

He was beside her, his presence sending quivers of excitement through her body.

'I phoned you just now.'

He was looking at her with a new intense expression that she couldn't believe. No more bitterness; no more suspicion; in fact, more than a hint of enormous pleasure.

She said unevenly, 'I heard it.'

'And didn't answer? Why not?'

His voice was amused and bright. She shook her head foolishly, aware only of his darkened eyes looking so intently into hers. He smiled. He wore the same old black jersey with the snagged arms, This was the Robert she recognised, and loved.

'And when I called at your flat in town you weren't there.'

'I told you, I was staying here for the week.'

The interrogation was exhausting her but the expression on his face was encouraging. She marshalled her confused mind.

'Why are you walking? Where's your car?'

'Sprung a puncture. I needed to get here, quickly and the footpath seemed the obvious way.'

She couldn't bring herself to ask the all-important question his words hinted at, so said

118

decorously, 'How did the exhibition go?'

Now his smile faded.

'Not badly. Some commissions and new contracts, but London! London was vile. Noisy, far too many people, no peace to work in. And Laura . . . '

'Yes?' Nicki prompted in a tiny voice.

He grinned unexpectedly.

'Laura was in her element. Meetings everywhere. So many contacts hidden up her elegant sleeve I thought my head would never stop whirling! I couldn't wait to get back to the peace and quiet of dear old Devon.'

Stopping, he picked up Nicki's hand and looked at it thoughtfully.

'And being on my own. And there's something else I learned about my difficult and egotistical character, something I have to thank you for, Nicki Bennett.'

'Me?'

'Yes, you, darling girl.'

Nicki gasped at what he'd called her.

'The present you left for me—the William Morris book.'

He was very close to her now, close enough for her to see the sparkle in his pale, vivid eyes, to see a gentler expression than the stern one she was used to. He was no longer the dead-pan Celt, stifling his feelings, but a man who was opening his heart—to her.

'Yes?' she whispered, her thoughts running wild, hardly hearing what he had to tell her.

119

'It was a wonderful present, Nicki. Good old William Morris brought me to my senses, made me realise that all I want is to live quietly, here, in the mill, making beautiful, useful things.'

He stopped abruptly, and then added, his voice deep and full, 'I don't think I would ever have realised it if you hadn't given me that book, my darling Nicki Bennett.'

Speechless, torn between disbelief and growing happiness, she could only stare at him. His face was calm now, handsome, and full of a new serenity that she wanted desperately to share. But in the confused background of her mind, certain images surfaced.

She caught hold of her emotions, and said, with a firmness she was far from feeling, 'So Laura isn't looking for a studio? She's still in London?'

Robert grabbed her hands in his and the strength of his energy sent a shock through her.

'No studio, no more Laura,' he said gently, looking deep into her eyes, and then added, slowly, and with a wry twist of his mouth, 'Laura was never anything more than a business go-between. Didn't you realise that?'

Nicki shook her head. Something wonderful was happening to her whole body. It felt lighter, more energised, so happy that she could hardly believe all she heard.

'Why didn't you tell me before?' she asked

lightly, and saw his smile broaden.

'Why didn't you ask me?' he countered, and they both laughed at the foolishness of the questions.

And then, for a moment, she saw his eyes darken, watched indecision etch his face, as he asked, so quietly that she hardly heard, 'And Leo?'

Spontaneously, she flung her arms around his neck, pulled his face down to hers, wanting only to blot out the very thought that there could be anyone in her world except him.

'Leo was a nightmare!' she murmured, adding, 'I've woken up now.'

She saw the tension break, glowed in the renewed warmth of the silvery eyes, and was able to laugh again, as he said, 'And we'll make our own dreams from now on,' before kissing her on the tip of her nose.

With Robert's hand gripping hers, they turned, as if with a single thought, and walked back along the footpath, towards the mill. Robert was full of plans now, ideas for using the insurance money to make the millhouse habitable and then return to his work there. Nicki listened, her own thoughts mingling with his.

'And the rest of the buildings?' she asked, when he paused for breath. 'If you're not going to sell, what will happen to them?'

By this time they had reached the lane and walked into the courtyard, standing, looking at

121

the old stones alight with the frail rays of the setting sun. Robert turned to her.

'Your father,' he began, and then stopped, his expression suddenly serious. 'I have something to ask you,' he said slowly.

'What is it?'

'It's important.'

Her mind raced. What had Dad said to him? Were there strings attached to the donation Dad wanted to make towards the restoration of the mill? Surely he wouldn't have done anything like that? But he had guessed how she felt about Robert. No, no, it wasn't possible! Yet Robert was looking at her so intently that she could almost believe anything. Suddenly words formed in her mind, and spoke themselves.

'And I have an important question for you, Robert.'

She would say it first. At least it would relieve her from this terrible suspense. Robert's face lifted, and he smiled.

'Well?'

'I want to be here in the mill, with you. Please?'

There, it was out! They stared at each other in silence and it seemed to Nicki that this was the worst moment of her life. If he rejected her, then she must surely wither away. But the tense expression on his face was fading. A tender smile replaced it, and then his arms were about her. She was pulled close, almost

122

stifled by the pressure of his hands around her body.

'But that's exactly what I was going to ask you,' he muttered into her hair. 'Trust a liberated woman to get in first!'

And then they were laughing together, seeing in each other's eyes the deep commitment both longed for. Slowly Robert lifted her face towards his, and they kissed, and Nicki knew that, at last, she was in the place she had longed to be since first they met. Minutes later, breathlessly, she freed herself and asked another question.

'What about Dad? I know he wants to give something to the mill. What were you going to say?'

Robert grinned.

'Before I was so rudely interrupted? Only all he said was that it's important that we get the mill wheel working very soon.'

His eyes were abruptly sombre, and she understood.

'In case he suffers a relapse?'

Robert nodded. They walked slowly through the courtyard, stopping beside the overgrown wheelpit.

'If I gave all my time to this, I could get the paddles repaired quite quickly,' he said thoughtfully.

'But the leat—it's not flowing.'

'Your dad's donation could deal with that. I'll get on to the water authority first thing

123

tomorrow.'

Hand in hand, they inspected the ruined timber of the wheel, and Robert turned to smile wonderingly at her.

'You understood about the wheel, right from the start, didn't you? You thought of it as a symbol of life.'

Nicki nodded.

'Like you, and Rowan, I knew, if it turned again, things would be right for me.'

She leaned against him, smiling up into his intent eyes.

'Now, it will turn, and everything will be right, for us.'

'And for Harry?' Robert asked gently.

Nicki sighed, but met his gaze honestly.

'We must hope, and help him to fight,' she answered simply. 'It's all we can do.'

CHAPTER SEVEN

'May Day,' Rowan called joyfully, dancing around the garden at Rose Cottage, carrying a nosegay of forget-me-nots, tulips and polyanthus. 'Time to celebrate summer! Come on, Nicki, let's take Mr Bennett home so that he can see.'

'Sh!' Nicki said rapidly, finger to her mouth. 'Don't tell him! It's meant to be a surprise.'

Rowan nodded, instantly quietened.

'Right. I'll go on home and tell Dad you're coming. By the time you and Gee get Mr Bennett into the car and down the lane, everything'll be ready.'

Tucking the small posy into her waistband, she grinned, waved a hand and ran off down the path.

Nicki found Gee fussing over Harry in the kitchen.

'Had your tablets? Feel OK? All the better for that good night's sleep?'

Harry Bennett cocked a grey eyebrow at her and smiled lovingly.

'You know, my sweet, you'd make a much better patient than I do! Always on the alert to my signs and symptoms!'

Gee brushed the top of his head with her lips as she went into the hall to fetch his anorak.

'You sure do say the nicest things, old man! Now, come on.'

Returning, she levered him out of the chair and into the jacket.

'We have a date. Let's get a move on.'

Nicki followed them through the front garden, towards the parked LandRover, watching Dad's slow steps, and forcing herself to keep hope at the forefront of her mind. The doctor said he was doing well, at the moment. She accepted that Dad's future was still uncertain, but during the last two weeks, since she and Robert had come together, her mind had grown wings. A new philosophy of life had been kindled, and now she knew that happiness could bring amazing and unexpected benefits.

What had Robert said yesterday, when she returned from her week back at work in London?

'Even when you're away, darling girl, I can still feel you here.'

Just as his strength and warm smile remained with her in town, driving through traffic or relaxing, alone in the evening, in her lonely flat. It was as though a thread connected them, through time and space.

Nicki smiled wryly to herself. Mysterious indeed! But she was able, these days, to believe in things hitherto pushed away. And now, something was about to happen which she knew would be in tune with her new thoughts.

Gee drove carefully down the thickly-hedged, twisting lanes, and Nicki smiled, recalling the former devil-may-care manner of her stepmother's progress. But then, Gee had changed in so many ways, as, indeed, she herself had done, for the better, she hoped, grinning at her father's curious face when he asked, for the third time, 'Where are you taking me?'

'Ask no questions you'll be told no lies!' she said brightly.

'The mill. Yes, I had a feeling!'

126

Harry leaned forward with enthusiasm as Gee parked the vehicle in the courtyard. As he got out, he put a hand on her shoulder and whispered something. Nicki saw Gee's smile flash, wondered at the sideways glance in her direction. But then Robert and Rowan were there with smiles and warm greetings. Rowan ran to Harry's side, linking her arm with his.

'In a minute,' she gabbled, 'you can come in for coffee, and some brilliant muffins I've just made, but right now you've got to stand still and watch something!'

Harry sounded resigned.

'All my women do is order me about,' he complained, but his eyes twinkled, and Rowan hugged him excitedly.

Then she turned to look at Robert, standing with his arm around Nicki, chatting to Gee.

'OK, Dad! Ready to go.'

Robert smiled at Nicki and took her hand.

'The big moment,' he said quietly.

'The great moment we've all been waiting for. Go on, love,' she replied.

Robert walked away, disappearing behind the wheelpit and the overgrown bushes that marked the boundary of the millhouse.

'What's happening exactly?' Gee asked, and Nicki said, 'He's opening the sluice gate. Watch.'

She looked back at her father, a few feet away, standing with Rowan's arm supporting him.

'Dad,' she said a little huskily, 'this is for you.'

There was a moment's silence, and then they all heard a strange, rushing noise. Water began to pour down the newly-dug leat bed. At first it was just a trickle, then, as its voice grew louder, so its power increased, until it was a strong, noisy current, flowing fast towards the wheel.

Nicki held her breath. By now Robert was back at her side and she grabbed his hand. They smiled, understanding and sharing this all-important achievement. A new sound joined the music of the rushing water—a rumble and creak of wheezing, aged timbers coming to new life, and then Harry's voice broke the enchanted moment.

'The wheel! It's turning!'

With one accord, they looked at him, saw an expression of great happiness flower on his pale face, and felt an answering joy. Gee walked across and kissed him, and then said, 'When we're in the cottage you can come and look at it every day,' she said tenderly.

Nicki, joining them, asked curiously, 'What's this about the cottage?'

'You're not the only one with a surprise, young lady.' Harry chuckled. 'Gee and I are buying old Archie's cottage from Robert.'

He grinned at the look of surprise on her face.

'So that we can keep an eye on you!' Then

he added, 'Not fair to keep Rachel from renting out her holiday cottage, we thought, and we like it down here. So, we move in at the end of the month.'

'That's wonderful, Dad. I'm delighted. And I'm glad you're so pleased about the wheel.'

She glanced admiringly at Robert.

'Robert's been working long hours on restoring all the paddles and getting the machinery going again. He wouldn't let anyone else do it.'

Harry didn't answer at once. He stood a little straighter in the warm sunlight, and looked about him. All the people he loved were here, in the place he loved. What more could he want? He smiled at Rowan beside him, then at Gee, watching him like a hawk; at Robert, whose strong arm encircled Nicki's waist, before moving back to the water wheel.

It turned now with a regular rhythm, its voice filling the quiet morning, the paddles scooping and releasing the flowing leat. Then, catching Nicki's eye, he knew instinctively what she was thinking. The restored waterwheel was a source of power, pumping out energy and bringing new life to the ancient mill and all who lived within and near it. It was a symbol of life itself.

Again, he looked around the faces watching him so intently, before smiling with great serenity, and saying what he felt was in all their hearts.

'Life goes on, doesn't it?' And then, huskily, to mask his deep emotion, he grinned at Rowan and whispered, 'What did you say about muffins? Lead on, dear child, I'm right behind you.'